NEIL YOUNG

A LIFE IN PICTURES

THIS IS A CARLTON BOOK

Published in 2012 by Carlton Books
an imprint of The Carlton Publishing Group
20 Mortimer Street
London W1T 3JW

A CIP catalogue record for this book is available from the British Library.

ISBN 978-1-84732-965-3

Editorial Manager: Roland Hall
Art Editor: James Pople
Design: A+E
Picture Research: Ben White
Production: Claire Halligan

Printed in Dubai

The publishers would like to thank the following sources for their kind permission to reproduce the pictures in this book.

Alamy Images: 94br, /AF archive: 148, /Pictorial Press Ltd: 72

Barrie Wentzell: 44, 50, 58, 98, 100

Corbis: /Henry Diltz: 6, 43, 49, 55, 61, 62, 91, 24-5, 70-1, 80-1, 18-19, 52-53, 56-57, /Hans Klaus Techt/epa: 138, /Christopher Felver: 150, / Lynn Goldsmith: 113, /Rune Hellestad: 140, 143, /Michael Ochs Archives: 16, /Aaron Rapoport: 114, /Johannes Eisele/Reuters: 155, /Rick Wilking/ Reuters: 12-13,

Getty Images: 27, 86, 151, 84-5, /AFP: 154, /FilmMagic: 134t, /Andy Freeberg: 132, /Gamma-Rapho: 109, /MCT: 156, /Michael Ochs Archives: 4, 10-11, 23, 28, 31, 34, 42, 54, 60, 69, 73, 83, 94tr, 128, 134 , 36-7, 14-15, 20-21, 40-41, /Michael Putland: 82, 94tl, 101, /Redferns: 39, 45, 47, 48, 59, 65, 66, 67, 76, 90, 92, 93, 95, 96, 97, 99, 102, 105, 106, 115, 116, 120, 122, 125, 127, 131, 136, 137, 146, 153, 158, 74-5, 88-9, 32-33, 78-79, /Donald Weber: 159, /WireImage: 51, 110, 147, 160

PA Photos: /Mark Davis/AP: 145, /Mark Humphrey/AP: 152, /Matt Sayles/ AP: 157

Photoshot: /Michael Putland/Retna: 77

Rex Features: /Mark Large/Associated Newspapers: 144, /Andre Csillag: 135, /Everett Collection: 118, /Brian Rasic: 2, /Reinstadler: 130

Every effort has been made to acknowledge correctly and contact the source and/or copyright holder of each picture and Carlton Books Limited apologises for any unintentional errors or omissions which will be corrected in future editions of this book.

NEIL YOUNG

A LIFE IN PICTURES

COLIN IRWIN

CARLTON

CONTENTS

ONE DAY IN THE SUMMER OF 1966, Neil Young was visiting a fair in Hollywood with his long-time friend and colleague – Buffalo Springfield bass player Bruce Palmer.

Young was 20 years old and already acclaimed as a songwriter of rare and unusual inspiration. His "Nowadays Clancy Can't Even Sing" – a disquieting song with a willfully obscure and introspective lyric about an old schoolfriend who'd constantly been persecuted back home in Winnipeg – had somehow become Buffalo Springfield's calling card during their surprising emergence as the latest darlings in an extraordinary wave of young bands emerging from Californian counterculture. He was not yet the band's front man, and the others thought so little of his vocal talents that they didn't even let him sing lead on "Nowadays Clancy Can't Even Sing" – or indeed any of the other songs he'd written for their repertoire – but there was an elusive aura surrounding Neil that marked him out as the most charismatic member. An awkward loner, his gaunt looks, perennial air of melancholy and moody sense of isolation made him attractively mysterious – always a powerful allure to audiences – while his complete lack of awareness about his own appeal, or any apparent interest in exploiting it in the time-honoured fashion of would-be rock stars, set him even further apart.

Hanging out with Neil that day in Hollywood, Bruce Palmer turned to his friend only to find him thrashing around on the floor in ugly convulsions. The shock was profound for everyone concerned. Neil quickly recovered, but the attacks began to recur, even striking him onstage on a couple of occasions. Neil eventually came to recognize the symptoms – he would bolt offstage during live performances with the rest of the band

LEFT: Neil Young circa 1971 – lank hair, intimidating glower, melancholic air, classic checked shirt – you don't want to mess with this guy!

running after him. The band would usually find him convulsing in another part of the building.

It was some time before Neil was officially diagnosed with epilepsy, and there were those – even from within the band – who weren't convinced that the attacks were anything more than attention-seeking affectation. But attention-seeking was never an option for an artist who, far from craving the spotlight, recoiled from the trappings of fame and celebrity.

Neil Young, who gradually learned to recognize, control and manage the symptoms of his illness, is hardly the only musician or public figure to suffer from epilepsy ... Prince, Lindsey Buckingham, Jimmy Reed, Ian Curtis, Adam Horowitz of the Beastie Boys, and Mike Skinner of The Streets, not to mention historical figures like Napoleon, Julius Caesar, Socrates and Dostoyevsky have all suffered. Yet when people try to explain the weirdly eccentric and wayward forces of imagination that have contrived to make Neil Young such a ferociously unpredictable and enduring genius, then epilepsy is invariably invoked as a theory.

On the few occasions Young himself discussed the matter, he didn't entirely discount the suggestion that epilepsy may have played a role in whatever it is that makes him so individual, obliquely referring to some kind of parallel universe that envelops him when the seizures strike, leaving their own blurry alternative images, which are largely inaccessible to the rest of us. Inaccessible, yet fascinating...

That sense of elusiveness and enigma makes Neil Young not only one of the greatest artists of the modern era, but one of the most consistently compelling and baffling. Foolish is the critic who tries to second-guess what Neil might do next. And foolish perhaps, too, is the critic who attempts to deconstruct the complexities of an artist whose words always leave room for doubt, apparently even in his own mind.

Somehow, Young found a profound way of channelling his isolated role as one of life's outsiders into creative music and lyrical ambiguity. Endless study of Young's background in search of the clues to unmask the forces that drive him are bound to fail, for there are few obvious answers. And if Young ever finds those answers himself, he's certainly not inclined to share them.

Epilepsy is one convenient explaination, but there are numerous other contributory factors in Young's early life that could have shaped his music. The polio he suffered as a child, for example, nearly cost him his life and left doctors predicting he'd never walk again, dumping on Neil a legacy of mental scars perhaps more damaging than the physical ones which left him self-conscious about his scrawny body.

Next came the acrimonious break-up of his parents' marriage. The fallout had a knock-on effect on Neil during his teenage years – it alienated him from his father and left him somewhat in awe of his iron-willed mother.

And then there's the company he kept; an early adoration of Elvis; a consuming admiration for Dylan; the bar bands he played in around Winnipeg; the dazzling influence of the outrageous, eccentric Rick James (in one of his first serious bands, The Mynah Birds).

Neil Young was a man with a virile imagination. Restless in his spirit of adventure, he bulldozed through all of the tried-and-tested guidelines for a successful career; discarding perceived record company wisdom about marketing strategies, public image and audience expectation along the way.

Neil Young despised most of the music industry's cherished commercial values. He trailblazed a track, fuelled on the innocence of artistic ambition. Young was oblivious to the pitfalls that lurked for anyone blindly pursuing a singleminded course. For him it was never even an issue; success just came naturally.

Don't ask Neil to explain his strategy – he never had one. There was no masterplan; no well-trodden career path to follow. His story is full of left-field tangents that should have spelled artistic and commercial suicide, yet instead served to seal his legend.

Young has constantly changed direction, radically reinventing himself – not in the studied, self-aware manner of Bowie or Madonna – but in deeply unfashionable, unglamorous ways that have seldom seemed logical or made much sense on any level.

And yet Neil Young has influenced successive generations across nearly 50 dramatic years in a career encompassing 34 solo albums, with spectacular contributions to some of the most iconic bands of their day – Buffalo Springfield; Crosby, Stills, Nash & Young; and Crazy Horse – and a series of classic songs like "Helpless", "Mr. Soul", "After The Goldrush", "Heart Of Gold", "Old Man", "Tonight's The Night", "Rockin' In The Free World", "Harvest Moon" et al.

How is it that someone who cut his teeth performing on the Winnipeg folk circuit ended up with musical styles incorporating folk-rock, country, blues, soul and ballads? It's no surprise then that Neil Young inspired such laughably grandiose epithets as "pioneer of symph rock", "Godfather of Grunge", "guru of psychedelia", "alternative rock god", "arch experimentalist", or "the king of rock 'n' roll" (as eminent critic Kurt Loder once contentiously described him).

And what are we to make of the array of aliases and alter egos which populate Young's CV? There's Bernard Shakey, under which he indulged his love of filmmaking via movies like *Journey Through The Past*, *Rust Never Sleeps*, *Human Highway* and *Greendale*. And then there's Phil Perspective, Clyde Coil, Joe Yankee, Pinecone Young and Marc Lynch. Are they remnants of an artist consumed by his own many faces; or the adopted masks of an indecisive spirit?

Young fans have remained determinedly loyal in the face of change, leaping through the numerous hoops Neil laid out before them, while rarely agreeing on what constitutes the good, the bad and the unlistenable in this most rarefied of careers.

Rock acts tend to create their most exciting, challenging, ambitious and successful work in their 20s; perhaps their 30s if they are late starters. By the time they reach 40, however, the game is invariably up and they tend to lean on past glories to maintain their careers. Rock music has grown up with its pioneers over the last 50 years, yet it remains rooted in the rampant energy and fearless imagination of the young. For older fans, rock music plays like a soundtrack to a golden time in their lives.

These rules don't apply to Neil Young. He avariciously explored new rock ground through his 20s, 30s, 40s, 50s and 60s, with little concurrence among his hardcore fans about which of these eras was the most productive. Surely no other popular artist has been able to make their audience willingly follow them up such long and difficult slopes. Along the way, there have certainly been potentially terminal falls in Young's career, exacerbated by health issues, such as the brain aneurysm that threatened to end his career in 2005.

There are still those who swear blind that Buffalo Springfield were the greatest rock band in the history of the world; that they represent Neil Young's finest hour by default. Then there are those who talk of the 1970s Crosby, Stills, Nash & Young album *Déjà Vu* – and specifically its classic song "Helpless" – in such hallowed terms that you'd think Young has never written anything better.

Other Young fanatics point to his seminal early 1970s solo albums *After The Goldrush*, *Harvest*, *On The Beach* and *Tonight's The Night*. The song "After The Goldrush" – originally written as part of the soundtrack to a movie that was never made – is, after all, still one of the most iconic and evocative songs to emerge from that richly productive Californian era. And if anyone doubted the claims of Young's supporters that he, more than anyone else, reflected the mood of a generation in those troubled times, then "Ohio" (written in the aftermath of the appalling student massacre at Kent State University) had the power to convince them otherwise.

Young's ability to mirror society through song continued to great effect on *Harvest* – an album revealing difficult truths in uncompromising fashion – that rocketed the man to international fame. One of its songs, "The Needle & The Damage Done", was written in response to the heroin addiction that would later claim the life of Neil's friend – Crazy Horse band mate Danny Whitten. It also brought Neil his only No. 1 single – "Heart Of Gold" – a consummate, yearning love song with bittersweet resonance, which its maker later publicly denounced due to its unwanted impact on his public image. "That song put me in the middle of the road," Neil commented scathingly. "Travelling there soon became a bore, so I headed for the ditch. A rougher ride but I saw more interesting people there."

If *Harvest* brought Young stardom and acclaim, it didn't bring him peace or happiness. The album triggered a departure into far darker songwriting territory, as Neil bleakly observed a world around him where drugs reigned supreme, the music industry operated on shallow morals, and America was being run by the odious "Tricky Dicky" Nixon. Young had felt the effects of fame and celebrity, and they nearly choked him.

Young started to make dauntingly heavy material that would divide opinion wherever he went. His record company therefore delayed the release of his subsequently acknowledged classic album *Tonight's The Night* for two years, causing him to lose chunks of his audience, much to their dismay.

Neil's music was shaped by ups and downs in his personal life: the guilt he felt over the drug deaths of Danny Whitten and roadie Bruce Berry; his relationship and subsequent break-up with actress Carrie Snodgress; their son born with cerebral palsy; a second disabled child; battles with band members and record companies; legal disputes. And as the dark clouds swirled over his personal life, Young's music descended into a series of seemingly barren tunnels.

The '80s are widely considered Young's "lost years" as a result, yet, while most careers are measured in terms of commercial success, it's an equation that never quite washes with Young. For everyone who dismisses the vocoder/electronica overload of *Trans*; the rockabilly covers album *Everybody's Rockin'*; the country swing of *Old Ways*; or the synth rock of *Landing On Water* or *Life* as unforgivable indulgences; there are dedicated fans that still hail them as neglected classics. Sales bombed, and debates raged about whether Young's experiments expressed a sincere desire to explore unfashionable parts of music or if he was just being perverse. His record label Geffen certainly thought it was the latter, suing him for recording music it considered unrepresentative of himself.

It all adds to the myth of a confusing but perennially fascinating character who came storming back at that end of that decade with the massive hit "Rockin' In The Free World" to once more become both a serious commercial proposition, and a thorn in the side of the establishment and sometimes his own friends too.

In April, 1994, one of the biggest rock stars of a newer era – Kurt Cobain of Nirvana – put a gun to his head after leaving a suicide note that closed with the words "it's better to burn out than to fade away." This was a line from a song on Young's 1979 album *Rust Never Sleeps* – "Hey Hey, My My (Into The Black)".

The tragic event gave Young a new status as an antihero. It made him a patron saint of sorts for another generation of disaffected outsiders, earning him the dubious title of "Godfather of Grunge".

Who said they were constantly a band at war? All smiles early in the Buffalo Springfield project – left to right: Richie Furay, Stephen Stills, Dewey Martin (front), Bruce Palmer, and "the man who couldn't sing", Neil Young.

Neil's regeneration has continued apace ever since. Through his 50s and into his 60s, he's remained one of the ultimate enigmas – inspiring, bewildering, shocking, delighting, trailblazing, politicking, frustrating, and thrilling in equal measure.

His ever-changing music has challenged our values (and at times our patience) with an attitude that's remained stubbornly individual and ferociously uncompromising. His songs mark him out as one of the true musical greats, while the contours of his life outline an extraordinary personality of rare courage and conviction, and great taste in hats.

Every picture tells a story, and Neil Young's story is colossal.

Colin Irwin

RIGHT: Folk singer, country rock maverick, pop crooner, protest singer, electro pioneer, Godfather of Grunge – Neil Young, a man of many hats.

CHAPTER 1
PRAIR

FORD
Comes Firs
SED CARS

WANDERLUST IS A POWERFUL OBSESSION. Well, it is if you're Mr. Neil Young.

The road has always been one of rock 'n' roll's primary sources of inspiration. Think of Chuck Berry singing "riding along in my automobile, my baby beside me at the wheel" on the classic "No Particular Place To Go" and you're halfway there. Another great example of wandering rock 'n' roll came when Berry belted out "Get your kicks on Route 66" – an anthem by jazz pianist and actor Bobby Troup, originally recorded in 1946 by Nat King Cole.

Wanderlust isn't limited to rock 'n' roll. After all, who could forget the Beach Boys surfing it up on "I Get Around"? And then there was Charles threatening to "Hit The Road Jack" in one of soul music's sweetest moments. All of these songs came about a long while before Bruce Springsteen's landmark rock album – one that embodies the idea of wanderlust – *Born to Run* in 1975.

Country and folk music is synonymous with the idea of wandering. Pioneers like Boxcar Willie, the Drifting Cowboys and Rambling Jack Elliott helped to usher in all of those train songs and the whole romantic myth of the hobo, while Roger Miller and Willie Nelson respectively eulogized about the romance of the highway in the cheerily nonchalant 1965 no. 1 hit "King Of The Road" and the classic "On The Road Again".

The blues is a whole other trip entirely. From Robert Johnson's legendary invocation of the devil on "Crossroad Blues", to Muddy Waters' enjoyably sleazy "Rollin' Stone", and John Lee Hooker's "Hobo Blues" where he lamented "when I first thought to hobo'in, I took a freight train to be my friend", the woes of life on the move are a staple element of the nefarious imagery that underpins such music.

Reaching right up from New Orleans to the Canadian border, Highway 61 not only has its own maze of mythology but also a spiritual resonance that runs through the heart of blues. There was the car crash that killed Bessie Smith in Clarksdale, 1937; then there was the glorification of the road as a symbol of escape and freedom by Mississippi Fred McDowell ("Lord if I happen to die baby 'fore you think my time has come, I want you to bury my body, yeah, out on Highway 61"); Robert Johnson even reputedly sold his soul at the Clarkdale crossroads where it intersects Highway 49.

It was small wonder that Bob Dylan announced his groundbreaking switch from folk to rock with an album titled *Highway 61 Revisited*. And Neil Young dreamed of hitting that same highway at the first opportunity.

For if there is any constant to be found among the inconsistencies in Young's life and music, it is his ongoing commitment to the adventure of travel, and the thrill of the road. Cars, highways, farewells, hellos, restlessness and passing strangers are the recurring subjects colouring Young's songwriting – they are the faithful, if unpredictable, kindle to his fiery muse. To a degree, these themes reflect the erratic contours of Neil's life, too, and few other artists invoke the seedy glamour of the road quite like a man with a longstanding passion for vintage automobiles and model railways.

"As soon as you change the scenery something happens and the words start coming," Neil said in an interview with *The Observer* in 2006. "Got to move on. *Anything* but staying in the same place. That ain't ever worked for me."

Restlessness remains embedded in Neil Young to this day. Growing up in Omemee, Ontario, his parents were constantly at loggerheads during a tempestuous marriage. His father Scott was a charmer; a sports writer with an eye for the ladies. The man had a good job – it took him all round the country – with a string of affairs to go with it.

Mother Rassy, a keen golfer with piercing black eyes, was a different character entirely – domineering, hard drinking, confrontational, wildly emotional, doggedly protective of her two sons, anti-authoritarian, and notoriously short-tempered.

The family were constantly on the move, from Omemee to Toronto to Pickering, before Scott and Rassy split up by the time Neil was 15. By then he'd already come through the trauma of polio (he was admitted to the isolation unit at a Toronto hospital as a chubby six-year-old and was wheeled out again after a week of agonizing treatment and mental torture as a terrified bag of skin and bones). They said he was unlikely to live. They said he certainly wouldn't walk again. But they were wrong. Neil developed a habit of proving people wrong.

When his parents divorced, Neil moved with his mother to Winnipeg to be close to her family, but brother Bob stayed in Toronto with their father. Already introspective, Neil's reaction to the move was to become even more non-communicative. He was later to renounce the popular assumption that he suffered a desperately melancholy childhood – a stereotype exacerbated by his quiet nature, and that familiar haunted expression that still plays on his face to this day, suggesting that the weight of the world hangs heavily on his drooping shoulders. It's hard to imagine that the family split didn't leave scars though.

Not that you'd know it from Neil's casual retelling of the story in his song "Don't Be Denied" from the 1973 album *Time*

LEFT: California dreamin'! Armed with a football, Furay's dodgy shirts and fedoras, Buffalo Springfield prepares to take LA by storm.

OVERLEAF: Original members of Buffalo Springfield stand in a psychadelic doorway just before the launch of their US hit "For What It's Worth".

Fades Away: "When I was a young boy my mama said to me, your daddy's leaving home today, I think he's gone to stay. We packed up all our bags and drove out to Winnipeg..." The song does, however, take on a more sinister edge as Neil recounts what awaited him at school in Winnipeg: "The punches came fast and hard, lying on my back in the school yard."

It would have been a confusing time for any young teenager arriving in the capital of Manitoba – hundreds of miles from the next city – in the early 1960s. They don't call it "the dead centre" of Canada for nothing. The word *dead* certainly has wry connotations.

Historically farming country, Winnipeg was originally a trading centre for the indigenous First Nation populations of Cree, Sioux, Ojibway and Assiniboine, who'd meet along the Red River. The arrival of the Canadian Pacific Railway there in 1881 triggered its rise to becoming Canada's seventh-biggest city, but its history would forever remain wrought with sadness: drought, the Great Depression of the 1930s, desperate unemployment, strikes, riots, flood disasters, energy crises, and severe, freezing winters that could cut in half the hardiest soul with a blast of wind (one environmental body even ranks Winnipeg as the coldest city in the world.)

By the time Rassy Young brought Neil there, Winnipeg was disparagingly referred to as "Hicksville", famous for its prairies, ice hockey, and precious little else. Small wonder then that Neil Young was already dreaming of Highway 61.

Neil lost himself in music, daydreaming at school about the time that he'd be up on stage, diligently drawing sketches of how the stage set would look. "I wasn't athletic, I just wanted to play in a band," he said in a BBC TV documentary. "I'd draw pictures of stages and the way they'd be set up. I spent a lot of time researching at that school."

Fuelling that dream was any scrap of music that made it through to the wilds of Canada in the early '60s, and that was quite a lot. The rock 'n' rollers were a massive influence on Neil: Elvis, Little Richard, Chuck Berry, Jerry Lee Lewis, Bo Diddley, and Fats Domino, as well as Afro-American singing groups The Chantels and The Monotones, and a pop trio from Olympia, Washington – The Fleetwoods.

Young discovered Johnny Cash early, and was also heavily into rockabilly, while harbouring a deep affection for the pop crooning of Roy Orbison and Del Shannon. Perhaps more surprisingly, Neil was beguiled by the English instrumental group The Shadows (better known as Cliff Richard's backing band) who had a string of catchy guitar hits like "Apache", "Wonderful Land", "Dance On"

RIGHT: You can take the boy out of the country, but you can't take the country out of the boy ... Neil Young, we're talking to you!

and "Foot Tapper". Neil confessed later that he was so smitten by them that he even imitated their notoriously unsophisticated dance steps.

Californian surf groups also influenced Neil. Not just the Beach Boys, but The Ventures and The Fireballs. And the harder stuff like Link Wray, whose extraordinary 1958 hit *Rumble* revolutionized the notion of electric guitar with its distorted power chords. "That was real primitive rock 'n' roll," commented Young. "It was the beginning of grunge."

Young's most direct influence, though, came from one of the few Winnipeg musicians to achieve widespread recognition at the time, Randy Bachman. Later to have a massive international hit with his song "You Ain't Seen Nothin' Yet" with the band Bachman-Turner Overdrive, Bachman was something of a superstar in Winnipeg. He played finger-picking guitar in Al & The Silvertones and Chad Allen & The Expressions, before hitting the big time as The Guess Who, who scored a No. 1 hit in Canada with a cover of Johnny Kidd & The Pirates' "Shakin' All Over". In his mid-teens, Neil got to see Randy Bachman play guitar on a regular basis, up close and personal. It touched him so deeply that he instinctively knew his own destiny was to be up on that stage.

Neil's first instrument was a plastic ukulele, and he slowly graduated to bigger and better ukes. It wasn't such a random introduction to playing music as it might seem, and was actually quite common in Canada, ever since a man called J. Chalmers Doane had introduced a radical new education programme fostering musical literacy by supplying schools right across the country with cheap and cheerful ukuleles. Fellow Canadian and kindred spirit Joni Mitchell had a similar introduction via the trusty ukulele.

After the uke, guitar was the natural jump, and once Neil had picked up his first guitar he couldn't put it down. It was a Harmony Monterey, which cost him about $30, he later recalled. Neil had a couple of lessons, but mostly he sat in his bedroom for hours on end working out the chords to his favourite Shadows and Danny & The Juniors tunes, and once he'd got the basics of playing, he started writing his own songs. And then, of course, he wanted his own band. As you do…

Neil's first school band was called The Jades which, disappointingly, wasn't even remotely embarassing. Rock stars' first bands should always have ridiculous names, like Blood Sledge Electric Death Chickens or Concrete Octopus or Holy Mary Mother Of Bert or New Riders On The Minimum Wage or Suicide Shrimp Fiasco (all real bands, by the way). But The Jades? Far too sensible by half. They didn't deserve to get anywhere … and didn't.

In The Jades, with Neil, was one Ken Koblun, who was to remain as Neil's faithful bass-playing lieutenant in a variety of short-lived bands that followed, with equally dull names such as The Stardusters, Twilighters, and The Classics, before they really settled into it as The Squires (another bad name, but at least they wore uniforms).

Naturally, Neil was the unequivocal leader, endlessly writing new material, sacking anybody who transgressed or didn't appear to be taking the band seriously enough, playing gigs at various venues all over Winnipeg, and generally making his presence felt. Which is odd, considering that the rest of the time Neil was mostly a moody loner plagued by insecurities who wouldn't say boo to a goose. But give Neil a guitar and a mission to become a rock star and he was a man possessed.

Friends of Neil's from that period in Winnipeg spoke of him being far older than his years, and it was true. Looking at pictures of Neil in his youth, he always appeared knowingly wizened. The man didn't live up to his family name.

Maybe it was Neil's disconnection with his father that he rarely saw since the move to Winnipeg; or maybe the devil that had given blues legend Robert Johnson godlike guitar skills in exchange for his soul had found his way across the Canadian border and struck a deal with Neil. Whatever the reason, Neil Young had rock 'n' roll coursing through his veins, and nothing was going to stop him from achieving his dreams of rock stardom that he had every day at Earl Grey Junior High School.

Neil had to wait quite a while to live his dreams, however. The Squires got to make the odd recording, and even had a minor local hit with the poppy "The Sultan" backed with a darker number "Aurora". Yet, far from being happy with this mini-breakthrough, the perfectionist in Young had already risen to the surface and was in chastising mode, muttering complaints about the sound quality and the general crudeness of the record.

Then came The Beatles. Canada was not immune to Beatlemania, and the "Liverpool effect" had a huge impact on all musicians, Neil Young included. He'd previously set his heart on only being a guitar hero, but The Beatles changed everything. Overnight it practically become law for every aspiring young band to include a healthy crop of Beatles covers in their set, and The Squires were no exception. Never mind the Shadows, The Beatles had moved the goalposts, and Neil realized that if he was

OPPOSITE: Beatles haircut, epic sideburns, tassled jacket … Young contemplates fame.

going to get anywhere, being a guitarist wasn't sufficient; now he had to be a singer too.

Reports of Neil's early singing attempts vary, from vaguely acceptable to totally unlistenable, but by then, Bob Dylan's nasal twang had careered over the horizon, so it didn't matter. Nobody in their right mind could claim Dylan was a technically good singer, but that wasn't the point. Lyrics were suddenly everything and nobody gave a fig about perfect pitch anymore. Folk music, apparently, was the future.

It was perhaps inevitable that Neil would drop out of school to follow his dream. It's what you do when you want to be irresponsible and chase something that everyone else says is out of reach. Everybody tutted and tried to talk him out of it, but Neil's rebellious streak was now rampantly ascendant, and his heart ruled his head.

He decided to leave Winnipeg and conquer Canada, hitting the road with a revamped Squires, who had been renamed Neil Young & The Squires. They started complementing their full-on rock with the fashionable folk references of the day – Neil adding harmonica to his skills in honour of Dylan.

They got a residency in Fort William, and slowly but surely evolved into a competent show. They learned to connect with the crowd; structure sets; develop harmonies; and rev up audiences. When things really heated up, Neil would drift into a trance-like frenzy, extending the instrumental breaks incessantly, like he'd lost complete control and was going to remain in the same state thrashing his guitar in demonic fashion for the rest of the night. It's a trait that's since become very familiar to hardy Young fans.

This was the period, too, when Neil's songwriting really found its range, with songs like "Nowadays Clancy Can't Even Sing", "Don't Pity Me Babe" and "Sugar Mountain". He wasn't alone, having become friendly with Joni Mitchell, who was taking her early steps on a similar journey. Meanwhile, Canada's own musical soul had been given a big lift by Ian Tyson, whose anthemic song "Four Strong Winds" – recorded with his wife Sylvia – had become an international folk hit. Maybe Canada wasn't such a backwater after all…

Neil's self-belief grew. The singer-songwriter path seemed to be the way to go, and Toronto was where it was all happening. And that's where, one day, Neil Young unceremoniously split from The Squires with no warning, no real explanation, and no apparent logic. That was just his way. He decided he didn't need them any more.

On a 12-string guitar, Neil started playing solo for the first time, trying to infiltrate Toronto's lively folk club scene. But it didn't pan

LEFT: Young's first big song "Nowadays Clancy Can't Even Sing" was inspired by a victimized acquaintance back in Winnipeg.

out the way he'd hoped. Permanently broke, Neil slept wherever he was offered a bed for the night, and blagged whatever gigs he could get. Which weren't many, but it was all part of his rock 'n' roll education.

Even now, though, you have to wonder about the surreal twist of fate which deposited Neil Young in a band with Rick James. You couldn't imagine any two characters less alike. Outrageous and flamboyant, James – who fancied himself as a black Mick Jagger – had absconded to Toronto from Buffalo to avoid reprisals after going AWOL from the US Navy, and was camping it up in black leather and yellow turtleneck tops as part of a blazing act called the Mynah Birds (previously known as the Sailor Boyz).

Finding themselves without a guitarist one day, the Mynah Birds chanced upon Neil Young in desperate need of a gig. It was a marriage made in a circus. The intense, would-be rock star Neil Young was clearly ill-prepared to join the 100mph party show that was Rick James and the Mynah Birds, but needs must and, as bizarre as it sounds, the two opposites found some sort of left-field common ground.

This epic meeting of minds and hearts would have made a great movie: Young and James apparently got on like a house on fire; they built an unlikely rapport on stage; they sang harmonies; they even started writing songs.

Neil was happy. James may have been the dominant force (which couldn't have been easy for his control freak partner to swallow) but Young managed to put his ego on hold long enough for both of them to get along fine, both onstage and offstage. Young and James were a popular act – they were signed to Motown, the gigs were working, and they were making money. A white rock act with a black lead singer … what could possibly go wrong?

The Navy caught up with Rick James, that's what went wrong. They tracked him down and arrested him in the studio just as the Mynah Birds were starting work on their album, shipping him back to the States to face the music, which turned out to be a year in a naval prison.

It was the end of the Mynah Birds, and Young was rudderless again. He teamed up with the Mynah Birds bass player, a certain Bruce Palmer, trying in vain to get work in Toronto coffee houses. These were soul-destroying times and, penniless once more, Young decided something drastic had to be done.

Dylan had released "Like A Rolling Stone", the press were telling everyone that the Byrds had invented folk-rock after they topped the charts worldwide with their cover of Dylan's "Mr. Tambourine Man", and Young then decided, once and for all, that he had to get out of Canada.

It had been part of Neil's vision all along to go to the States to make it. Even before he'd formed The Squires, Neil had been investigating the logistics of both filling in the forms for legal entry and sneaking across the border illegally. Having failed to make it in Toronto – let alone the rest of Canada – now was the time to go for broke. It was now or never.

The road called, so Neil and Bruce Palmer sold all their worldly goods to buy a 1953 Pontiac hearse, rounded up some friends, and headed for the border. The travellers were on their way: destination California.

STOP, HEY WHAT'S THAT SOUND?

California in the mid-1960s was the stuff from which music dreams were made. Aspiring rock stars from all over North America flocked to LA and San Francisco in hot pursuit of the idyllic illusions created by the Beach Boys' surf sound and the whole Jan & Dean image of a teen utopia.

When the Mamas & the Papas hit the big time with "California Dreamin'" in 1966, it established the west coast as the Mecca of the hippy/psychedelic era. California went on to dominate the contemporary pop world, shifting the whole axis of youth culture with an irresistible mantra of "peace and love". Anybody who wanted to be somebody *had* to be in California. It was where ideas germinated, dreams began, old values meant nothing, and bands formed. The centre of the music universe moved almost overnight from Lancashire, England to California, USA. This was the new, officially happening capital of rock, where deals were struck and stardom was touchable.

Dylan had obliterated the rule book with "Like A Rolling Stone", the term "folk rock" was on everybody's lips, and a new era had begun. Broke and dispirited playing in Toronto bars, Neil sensed the change in the wind, and once more believed that his long-held dream of making it in the States would become reality.

It was March, 1966, and, travelling in style in the Pontiac hearse he'd bought with the proceeds of the now-redundant Mynah Birds equipment he'd flogged, Neil Young, along with Bruce Palmer and friends, headed for Los Angeles.

Despite lacking strategy or a gameplan, Young and Palmer talked airily of the band they planned to form once they arrived in LA. They'd met a couple of guys in Canada who were now living there, and figured they might hook up with them. The

RIGHT: Neil's great contemporary, fellow Candadian, kindred spirit and early supporter, Joni Mitchell.

duo were just relying on their wits, the free spirit of the day, and serendipity, to make it happen.

They made it illegally across the border, reaching LA unscathed. There they named their band after a make of steamroller: Buffalo Springfield.

It's strange now to contemplate that Neil Young – so strong, independent, determined, willing, and controlling – was never the front man or leader of the first band to launch him into the international arena.

Then again, Neil was in a group full of other guys who were strong, independent, determined, willing, and controlling. Not least a certain Mr Stephen Arthur Stills – Young's animated and vitriolic sparring partner, and occasional nemesis.

To most casual observers of the day, Stills was the undisputed leader of Buffalo Springfield. An intense perfectionist that knew exactly what he wanted, Stills was loud, flamboyant, smiley, gruff-voiced and supremely self-confident; hell-bent on pursuing the quickest route to success. He'd already come within a whisker of joining The Monkees – the manufactured teen stars of the 1960s who'd become a pop phenomenon on the back of a very silly yet eminently likeable TV series – but Stills had been denied this particular slice of early adulation (Peter Tork took his place).

Stills and Young first met when Stills was on tour in Canada with The Company, one of a series of short-lived bands he'd formed along the way that never grew beyond bar-room status. Deciding that his destiny to be a star must be awaiting him on the west coast, Stills headed for California, summoning Richie Furay – another young singer/guitarist he'd met along the way – to join his new band.

Legend has it that Stills and Furay were driving around Los Angeles in a white van looking for other musicians to join their band, and pulled up at a red light on Sunset Boulevard. They glanced across at the strange vehicle travelling in the opposite direction – a hearse. Stills only knew one man who drove a hearse ... and he knew Neil Young was in town.

The way Neil told it later: *he* was in LA actively seeking Stills (as opposed to Stills seeking him), asking anybody and everybody if they knew where the man was. Neil was on the verge of giving up and heading for San Francisco when those fateful traffic lights turned red.

Buffalo Springfield still divides opinion, not least with Young himself. Stills, Richie Furay, Bruce Palmer, drummer Dewey Martin, and Young, were a motley crew of deeply diverse personalities, with plenty of conflict between them from day one. How could there not have been conflict given their characteristics?

Young was the brooding Canadian songwriter already wrestling with his own love-hate relationship about the idea of stardom. Texan-born Stephen Stills was the dramatic, arch-populist who desperately wanted it all and was determined to get it whichever way he could. Richie Furay, erstwhile front man of a folk trio in Ohio who'd previously played with Stills in the Au Go Go Singers, was lead singer on many Springfield tracks, and a livewire stage performer; another nominal leader. Young's loyal but idiosyncratic friend Bruce Palmer was a wild party animal offstage who turned his back on audiences when on it, yet he played bass with such passion that many observers identified him as the real power in the band. And then there was Canadian Dewey Martin on drums, bringing with him a considerable CV that included many Nashville sessions and gigs with Roy Orbison, The Dillards, Carl Perkins, and Patsy Cline.

Yet surely one of the great truths about rock 'n' roll is that the best bands are the ones at each other's thoats who try to kill one another on the road. It's only when relations and communications completely break down and the friction is gone that bands lose their explosive chemistry.

Things happened fast for Springfield (contrary to the myth, they didn't have to earn their dues and serve apprenticeships on the road). They played their earliest gigs in LA's hottest club, the Whisky A-Go-Go on Sunset Strip; they opened for the Rolling Stones at the Hollywood Bowl; they were swiftly off on tour supporting the band with whom they were sometimes compared, the Byrds. Yet, with a front line of three guitars, and Palmer and Martin providing a ferocious broadside with their bass and drums respectively, Buffalo Springfield were palpably different to anything that had gone before, and proved to be an instant sensation with audiences.

Internal jealousies soon festered, particularly between Stills and Young. Young was one of the main songwriters, but it was Furay who mostly sang his lyrics and, while Young was reluctant to assume any sort of leadership role in the band, tensions soon came to the fore. Young had little faith in his own singing ability, but he wasn't easy with the notion of standing around playing guitar while someone else hogged the spotlight singing one of his songs.

The band had reached its limits, and Young was a long way from being its primary creative force. He had become a gangly, indistinct presence at the back of the stage playing a white Gibson guitar, characterized by a long, dark trench coat, decrepit jeans, rampant sideburns, and a variety of interesting hats.

LEFT: America's answer to The Beatles? Neil Young's fateful encounter with Stephen Stills and Richie Furay in LA ended up as a marriage made in heaven ... and hell.

Of all the members of Buffalo Springfield, Young seemed the least likely to have a glittering 50-year career ahead of him, yet it was his songs that held most sway in the band. "Nowadays Clancy Can't Even Sing", the first single, was written by Young a year or so earlier and had been performed solo by Richie Furay ever since he'd heard the song when they'd met in New York. "Clancy" is a strange and complex song, but its unusual time changes and random themes of alienation and displacement – including a telling reference to the betrayal of a former girlfriend in Winnipeg – hit the mark, and characterized Young's identity as one of life's outsiders. "Who should be sleeping that's writing this song? Wishin' and a-hopin' he weren't so damn wrong."

"Clancy" was the band's first single, but it flopped miserably amid criticism that it was too long and obscure for mass consumption, and also because of its inclusion of the word "damn" in its lyrics, which scuppered its chances of airplay. In retrospect, the band might have fared better if their original choice of debut single – Stills' rather jauntier effort "Go And Say Goodbye" – hadn't been relegated to the B-side.

The single's failure was also indicative of Springfield's Achilles heel. They were a great live band that could never fulfil their potential in the studio. Much of the blame for this habitually falls on Charlie Greene and Brian Stone – the famed fast-talking management team who'd taken Sonny & Cher to the top, and whose subsequent control of Buffalo Springfield's professional fortunes extended to the studio.

Even while they were recording their debut album, Buffalo Springfield was falling apart. The band's internal arguments began to spill onto the stage, particularly due to Stills and Young. Much tension also stemmed from the band's concensus that, in the studio, Greene and Stone didn't know what they were doing. While Phil Spector was rewriting the book on production techniques, creating imposing layers to boom out of speakers in his famous Wall of Sound, the shallow music emerging from the mix on Buffalo Springfield's first album convinced the band that their records were the result of production by numbers. Relations between band and management collapsed amid standoffs about the group's demands for the album to be recut or even rerecorded, which fell on deaf ears.

And yet, that self-titled first album didn't bomb in the way the band gloomily predicted. Reviews were largely positive, and their fame spread because of it. If nothing else, the album included some interesting early Young songs, especially "Flying On The Ground Is Wrong", which was a late inclusion, ranking as his most revealing song of the period. Like two other Young songs on the album, it was sung by Richie Furay, but was very much Young's baby. Inspired by one of his favourite records – Roy Orbison's "Blue Bayou" – its barbed lyrics were clearly written by someone with an already jaundiced view of the rock industry.

Similarly, "Out Of My Mind" (one of Neil's songs that his band mates *did* let him sing) stemmed from Neil's distaste for the trappings of a world in which he was fast becoming entrenched. "All I hear are screams from outside the limousines that are taking me out of my mind," he sang. The band weren't riding around in too many limos at the time, and Young's anxiety and fear was palpable in the trembling and vulnerable vocals that would become his trademark. If "Flying On The Ground" marked Young's emergence as a caustic songwriter of rare depth, "Out Of My Mind" was his coming of age as a singer.

That first Buffalo Springfield album reached No. 80 on the Billboard charts, and while the band still believed that they were destined for greatness, they were still being ravaged by internal disputes. It was an outside influence – a Stephen Stills song – that dramatically changed their fortunes.

Complaints by residents and business owners about noise, disturbances and late night traffic coming from the long-haired revellers tumbling out of the Whiskey A Go-Go, Pandora's Box and other clubs on Sunset Strip – frightening off tourists – resulted in police invoking a 10pm curfew on the Strip. The demonstration that followed descended into a full-scale riot, inspiring Stills to commemorate the event with a new song "For What It's Worth".

Its infectious chorus "Stop children what's that sound?" boomed out of the radio in early 1967, resonating with the dawn of the psychedelic era, and becoming Buffalo Springfield's first hit single. Added to the band's hastily reissued debut album, it became the anthem for the new era of west coast culture.

Single success did nothing to assuage the growing antipathy between Young and Stills. Young wasn't part of the gang. He wanted rock stardom, but hated everything that went with it. Drugs were practically de rigueur in LA at the time, but Neil had no need for hallucogenic stimulation – what went on naturally in his head surpassed any drug trip.

Damaged by the onset of epileptic fits, Young was hospitalized for 10 days. He undertook intensive medical tests that left him troubled and exhausted. Bruised by rows with Stills and stand-offs with management, Young sat up all night and wrote his most significant song of the era – "Mr. Soul".

RIGHT: "All I hear are screams from outside the limousines that are taking me out of my mind..." sang Neil on "Out Of My Mind" as a solo career beckoned.

It left no doubts about his deep discomfort with his current fate. It was a darkly disquieting song built around a Rolling Stones riff that seemed to recoil against drugs, groupies and the whole rock-star culture, prophesying an uncertain future. Resulting directly from his health traumas, the song was even interpreted by some as a premonition of death but, as ever, Young's lyrics were too oblique for any clear meaning to be evident, and his own thoughts on the subject are typically vague and elusive.

Yet the song's sinister mystery is partly what makes it so compelling and powerful; the band invariably closed their live sets with increasingly frenzied versions of "Mr Soul". Sometimes Young would drift into perpetual thrash mode, where he seemingly couldn't extricate his hands from the guitar. And, more worryingly, the whole thing sometimes became so intense that it triggered a seizure.

When Young abruptly quit Buffalo Springfield in May, 1967, the song seemed oddly prophetic.

Given the band's dissatisfaction with the lack of studio expertise on their first album from producers Charlie Greene and Brian Stone, Atlantic Records guru Ahmet Ertegun decided to personally oversee the recording of the second. It didn't go well. Stills and Young largely insisted on taking control of producing their own songs, while Richie Furay was writing more and wanted his songs included. Meanwhile, there was further chaos, as Bruce Palmer's dangerous new appetite for rock 'n' roll excess resulted in marijuana charges and his temporary expulsion from the US back to Canada.

Then there was the not inconsiderable influence of the formidable Jack Nitzsche, the outspoken producer who'd originally made his mark writing epic arrangements for Phil Spector's Wall of Sound on hits like the Crystals' "He's A Rebel" and Ike & Tina Turner's "River Deep, Mountain High".

Convinced from the outset that Young was the real talent in Buffalo Springfield, Nitzsche encouraged him to explore his own course, bringing him into the studio alone to work on more expansive arrangements of his songs. Nitzsche convinced Young that his music deserved more and, in the wake of the release of The Beach Boys' epochal *Pet Sounds*, and with The Beatles releasing their groundbreaking *Sgt Pepper's Lonely Hearts Club Band* album, Young wrote two more big songs, "Expecting To Fly" and "Broken Arrow".

Both subsequent recordings are marked by Nitzsche's ambitious orchestral scores, which caused consternation in some quarters. Their heavy sounds stood accused of eclipsing Young's lyrical subtleties, while the other members of the band were largely

---

LEFT: "I used to play in a rock 'n' roll band but they broke up, we were young and we were wild, it ate us up..."

excluded from the tracks. Singing harmonies, Richie Furay was the only other band member who featured on the lush ballad "Expecting To Fly", on the second Buffalo Springfield album. It was even released as a single, but it flopped, barely breaking into the Billboard Top 100.

"Broken Arrow" was even more ambitious, with its layers, overdubs and complex shifts in mood underlining the song's essence of fear and loathing (even including a fleeting extract from "Mr Soul"). To all intents and purposes, it was the first serious song in a new solo career by Young. Pop music was suddenly becoming very highbrow and arty, and Neil Young wanted in.

Whether he meant to or not, Jack Nitzsche convinced Neil that he didn't need the rest of the band because they were holding him back.

So, irked that Stills' song "Bluebird" had been chosen ahead of "Mr. Soul" as the band's new single, Young, strung out on the valium he was taking to combat his seizures, walked away from it all before the second album *Buffalo Springfield Again* was finished. The rest of the band weren't thrilled by his timing – they had to forfeit an appearance on Johnny Carson's highly influential *The Tonight Show*, and Young also missed out on what would then have been the biggest show of his life alongside the likes of Janis Joplin, Jimi Hendrix, Otis Redding and The Who, in front of 55,000 people at the 1967 Monterey Pop Festival.

It was ironic that 1967 was heralded as the "summer of love", for there didn't seem to be much sunshine or romanticism in Neil's life at the time.

Despite the inclusion of three mighty Neil Young songs – "Expecting To Fly", "Broken Arrow" and "Mr. Soul" – most of the plaudits for Buffalo Springfield Again went to Stills for his big tracks "Bluebird", "Rock & Roll Woman" and "Everydays". Young had issues: his health; his distrust of the music industry; his rivalry with Stills; his lack of conviction about his vocal talent; his isolationist stance; his financial woes. The surprise wasn't that Young quit Buffalo Springfield in 1967, it was that he returned to the fold in time for the album's release.

Most people – including Young himself – now look back kindly on *Buffalo Springfield Again*, and regard it as Buffalo's finest hour. It was the album best received by the public and critics alike (apart from a reviewer from *Downbeat* magazine, who complained that they didn't have a sound of their own, and dismissed them as "the Bobby Darin of groups – ultimately the parts are greater than the whole and the album lacks focus"). Yet, it wasn't long before the simmering friction between Stills and Young reached boiling point again, with lots of stories surfacing about confrontations and face-offs on the road.

Both had seemingly given up on the idea of working meaningfully together again. Their new producer Jim Messina – who'd engineered the second album and was by now installed in the band as Bruce Palmer's regular replacement on bass – attempted in vain to keep the peace long enough for them to record their third album. It was a hopeless task, and by May, 1968 – barely two years since they formed, and in the wake of a damaging drug bust – it was all over for Buffalo Springfield.

Jim Messina and Richie Furay did manage to cobble up one more rather sad and unsatisfying album, *Last Time Around*, from the dregs of those disorganised recording sessions, to fulfil their commitment to the record label. But not one track featured every band member and, already thoroughly disillusioned, Young played only a minimal role in those sessions. He did, however, have the dubious honour of penning the band's farewell single "On The Way Home" (sung with Young's blessing by Richie Furay), in addition to a Furay collaboration "It's So Hard To Wait". Young's one lead vocal on the album was "I Am A Child" (on which drummer Dewey Martin was the only other band member who played). Neil didn't even stick around for the photo session of the album sleeve – his picture was pasted on later.

Nobody could have been too surprised by the outcome, except perhaps the Buffalo Springfield boss at Atlantic Records, Ahmet Ertegun, who cried when he heard the news of their split, still believing them to be one of the greatest bands of all time.

So what are we to make of this period in Young's career? To all intents and purposes it was a miserable time in his life, and yet much of the music he created still stands up to close scrutiny and might even be considered visionary or ahead of its time. Buffalo Springfield helped to pioneer country rock and were certainly a million times more exciting, challenging and influential than most of the related bands who came in their wake, like Poco, Loggins & Messina, and the Souther, Hillman, Furay band.

And despite everything, Young seems to recall those days with unexpected affection. He rejected various attempts along the way to get the band back together again, and couldn't quite bring himself to rejoin the circus when Springfield were inducted into the Rock and Roll Hall of Fame, yet he said all the right things in a fax readout at the proceedings: "The music Buffalo Springfield made, the times we had, will always be an important part of my life. I will always be grateful for coming of age during the mid-1960s, and it still means as much to me, now and forever. I close

LEFT: High jinks in the photo session for the *Buffalo Springfield Again* album sleeve.

my eyes, breathe deeply, open my soul and dream of the Buffalo Springfield."

Hmmm … is there a tongue-in-cheek element in those words? Surely not.

It may have been more of a nightmare than a dream when it was all kicking off around him, but time mellows everything, and Young clearly came to acknowledge that he couldn't have had a better grounding in the rigours and mayhem of life as a rock star than in the dysfunctional chaos and personal torture of this band at that time.

30 years after Buffalo Springfield split, Young started accumulating tracks for a chronological 4-CD retrospective box set that included several previously unreleased songs, which eventually saw the light of day in 2001, including notes that spoke well of the period.

Then there was the 2000 solo album *Silver & Gold,* which included the track "Buffalo Springfield Again" – a surprisingly nostalgic glance back at the madness: "I used to play in a rock 'n' roll band, but they broke up. We were young and we were wild, it ate us up." It also featured a whimsical reference to a possible reunion: "Like to see those guys again and give it a shot, maybe now we can show the world what we got. But I'd just like to play for the fun we had."

In an interview a few years later, Young was still ridiculing any notion of a comeback, likening talk of a reunion to "a monument with birds shitting on our heads – it wouldn't be right."

Yet, hey presto, against all odds it finally happened. In October, 2010, Neil Young stood shoulder to shoulder with Stephen Stills and Richie Furay once more to play two benefit concerts raising money for The Bridge – the school he founded in Hillsborough, California in 1986 to help severely disabled children communicate.

Drummer Dewey Martin had died the previous year and bassist Bruce Palmer passed in 2004, but old grudges were buried and, after one beautifully mournful treatment of "Nowadays Clancy Can't Even Sing" – one of the highlights – the gigs went well enough to persuade the participants that there was still life in the old Buffalo yet.

So with the places of Martin and Palmer taken by Joe Vitale and Rick Rosas respectively, Buffalo stirred once more in the summer of 2011 for a series of gigs in Oakland, LA, Santa Barbara, and Manchester, Tennessee.

They didn't kill one another. They didn't fight. They didn't try to outdo one another. They sounded good and they had a great time. Wearing his favourite tassled Indian jacket and a rather fetching boater hat highlighted by a sturdy black band, Neil was positively animated, chatting easily with the audience and stomping purposefully around the stage while trading fearsome licks with Stills.

Most of the biggies were there: "Mr. Soul", "Nowadays Clancy Can't Even Sing", "Broken Arrow", "For What It's Worth", "Burned", "Everybody's Wrong", "Hot and Dusty Roads", an elongated "Bluebird" climaxing with an impassioned guitar jam, and one of Young's most famous post-Springfield songs, "Rockin' In The Free World". As comebacks go, it was a rare triumph.

The demons had been cast aside and from his position of longstanding eminence, Neil clearly saw that the petty jealousies, squabbles and rivalry with Stills had driven them both to unimagined new heights both as guitar players and songwriters. Floundering around seeking the strength to survive in a period that routinely took its toll on many contemporaries certainly gave Neil the ammunition and strength of character to continue his onward journey with determination and vigour.

Neil Young found his voice in Buffalo Springfield. It may initially have been a whiney voice that was roundly ridiculed by many who heard it – including his bandmates at the time – but it's hard to see how Young would have progressed into the durable force he became without the Springfield experience. All the bitterness, fury, tantrums, health scares, excess, and disputes – not to mention the experience of studio techniques, and the undeniable influence and inspiration of the outstanding musicians who were his colleagues – had fuelled his solo career in waiting.

It was a seminal period in rock 'n' roll history that defined American culture. Dylan and the Byrds may have opened the door, but Buffalo Springfield eagerly powered through it to explore the potential of folk and country influences, with the considerable ammunition of twin guitars, and fierce drums and bass.

More than that, Buffalo Springfield was a significant marker for the uprising of west coast rock. It sounded the death knell of the hippy idyll, as American youth awoke to the cold, stark truths of a turbulent period in their history. The Vietnam war; the My Lai massacre and the battle of Saigon; the assassinations of Martin Luther King and Bobby Kennedy; student riots; the rise of black militancy; and the election of Richard Nixon to the White House.

With the American dream crumbling all around them, it was an apposite time for Buffalo Springfield to fall apart, leaving Neil Young to contemplate his next move…

PREVIOUS PAGES: Neil was always at his happiest in a swanky car.

RIGHT: Mr. Soul dumps his traditional farmhand look and tries out a dress shirt.

CHAPTER 2

EVERYBODY I LOVE YOU

BY THE TIME THEY GOT TO WOODSTOCK they were half a million strong and there was song and celebration. They were stardust, they were golden, and they had to get themselves back to the garden…

Joni Mitchell always had a way with words.

In rock mythology, Woodstock has an untouchable place at the top of the table. The legendary festival was held in upstate New York from August 15–18, 1969, and produced a hit movie (credited with saving Warner Bros from extinction; a glut of best-selling live albums; and an alternative culture. It remains one of the ultimate landmarks for the '60s generation.

Billed rather pretentiously as "An Aquarian Exposition: 3 Days of Peace & Music", the Woodstock Music & Art Fair (actually 43 miles from Woodstock) has long since achieved immortality in the public mindset. It was a core event that inspired a massive pilgrimage of beautiful people that came to represent the apotheosis of the hippy ideal.

The fact that there was a vehement local body of opposition to the festival underlined its importance as the poster event of underground culture, while the fact that it became free due to the difficulty in fencing and policing ensured the conservation of its freewheeling principles.

However, Woodstock was also a tough endurance test for those who braved horrendous traffic jams, fought their way through the intrusive crush of the massive crowds, and suffered the indignity of rain and mud.

In terms of sanitation, food supplies and shelter, Max Yasgur's 600-acre dairy farm up in the Catskills, close to the town of Bethel – a

LEFT: A rock star is born … sort of.

ABOVE: Young, Nash, Crosby and Stills.

Marlboro

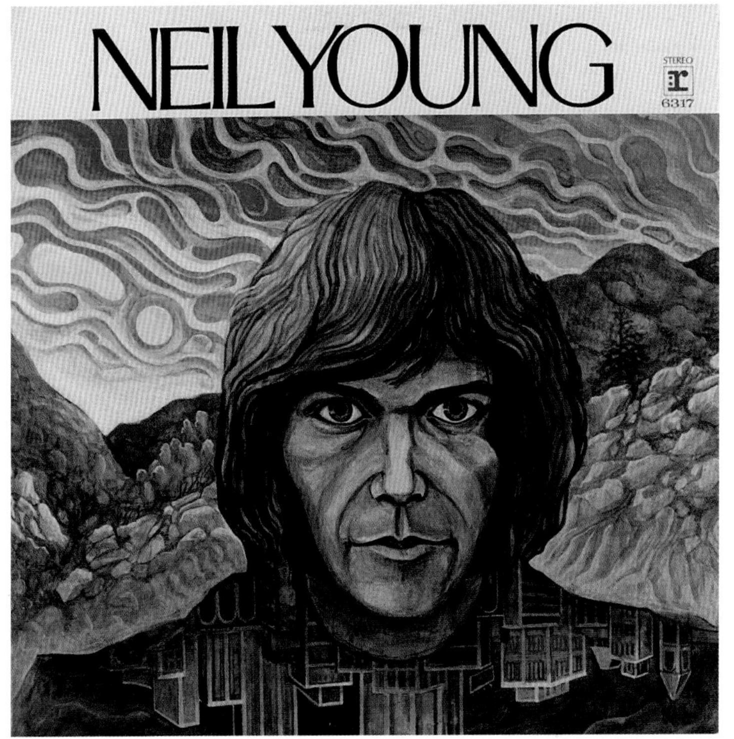

PREVIOUS PAGES: Young drove a hard bargain before joining Crosby, Stills & Nash. Tasteful fashion clearly wasn't part of the deal...

ABOVE: Sleeve of Neil Young's eponymous solo album in 1968.

LEFT: A supergroup is born. Left to right: Graham Nash, David Crosby, Neil Young and Stephen Stills work on material for their first album.

late choice of venue – was woefully ill-equipped for the influx of half a million hippies, beatniks, dropouts and just regular music lovers.

And yet, it *was* amazingly peaceful and good-humoured. There were two deaths, however – one from a heroin overdose and another when a guy sleeping in a hayfield was run over by a tractor – but the fears the locals had of mad youngsters with long hair running around rioting, looting and generally creating havoc didn't materialize, and the revellers sprinkled indelibly positive vibes all over society.

All the bands who gave a half-decent performance (and quite a few who didn't) were canonized as patron saints of a new era of sunshine and flowers, where everyone made love not war. And prominent among them were Crosby, Stills, Nash and Young.

The band were in exactly the right place at the right time, and they made the most of their opportunity with a performance and songs that seemed to fit the festival like a glove, which went a long way to cementing critics' claims that CSNY defined a generation.

If Neil Young had any regrets about missing out on the Monterey festival after walking out on Buffalo Springfield shortly before it took place, he didn't show it. But now he was at the heart of one of American rock culture's most seismic events as it unfolded.

Woodstock was only CSNY's second gig. Their first – undertaken after intensive rehearsals at Peter Tork's house – was at Chicago Auditorium on August 16, 1969, with Joni Mitchell opening. Two days later, they headed for Woodstock.

The Woodstock bill featured many acts who would later be considered the greatest and most influential of their era. The following eponymous movie captured defining performances from the likes of Richie Havens, Melanie, Country Joe & The Fish, John Sebastian, Santana, Janis Joplin, Grateful Dead, Sly & The Family

ABOVE: Crosby, Stills, Nash and Young pioneered the concept of stadium rock in the free world.

RIGHT: Neil took exception to the cameras at Woodstock.

Stone, The Who, Joe Cocker, The Band and Jimi Hendrix.

Crosby, Stills, Nash and Young played on the Sunday evening, sandwiched between Johnny Winter and the Paul Butterfield Blues Band, and most observers concurred that they took the festival by storm and were the best band of the whole weekend.

It's not a universally held view, however. Young was in such a foul mood that he refused to allow himself to be filmed, threatening to hit any cameraman who came near him with his guitar. Young had his name wiped off the credits of the subsequent live album. His take was that the whole thing was a sellout, and he was repulsed by Stills lapping up the huge crowd and playing to the gallery.

Yet Stills also declared himself unhappy with the band's performance, saying that nerves had got the better of them, and that they played out of tune most of the time.

So how is it their performance at Woodstock came to be perceived as the set that summed up not only the whole ethic of the festival, but that it also captured the mood of the time? There wasn't anything particularly remarkable in the set that night: it opened with "Suite: Judy Blue Eyes", then moved into a cover of The Beatles' "Blackbird", followed by "Helplessly Hoping", Crosby's "Guinnevere", and then the big hit "Marrakesh Express". They played the old Buffalo Springfield favourite "Bluebird", but there were only two Young songs in the whole thing: "Mr. Soul" and "Wonderin'".

Yet, flawed as the performance was, the band came out of it smelling of roses. Crosby, Stills and Nash had at least thrown themselves into the occasion with everything they had: Stills and Crosby both wheeling passionately around the stage; Nash delivering those extraordinary, soaring harmonies; the ever-enigmatic Young staring morosely at the crowd, thrashing his guitar, every inch the charismatic, wayward maverick.

They had a good evening slot and they caused a sensation, winning one of the warmest and most heartfelt reactions of the weekend from the sodden masses, and earning endless plaudits from their contemporaries. "It was their time – they represented the Woodstock sound," said Grace Slick.

The real reason their name became seamlessly etched into the whole legend of Woodstock, however, was due to Michael

Wadleigh's eponymous movie, edited in part by Martin Scorsese, which hit screens the following year.

If Stills had spent the set playing to the cameras, as Young thought, it clearly worked. With the dodgier musical moments resolved in the editing suite, Crosby, Stills and Nash dominated the big screen, and their meticulous harmonies and clashing guitars seduced audiences in movie theatres all over America. They'd played to half a million at the festival, but they reached a lot more than that through the miracle of celluloid.

It sealed a legend that, over the years, inspired them to reform whenever the whole thing inevitably fell apart. And the fact that CSNY were such a disjointed and often cataclysmic success story put them in the small pantheon of bands credited with shifting the sands of music in a specific time and place. Particularly when Neil Young became involved.

Neil Young is a man of many contradictions. This is the guy who once refused to join Graham Nash in a benefit concert for some leftist cause or another on the grounds of artistic independence; the same guy who ridiculed Tricky Dickie Nixon, but came out in unexpected support for another right wing Republican leader Ronald Reagan, before howling *Let's Impeach The President* in the direction of George W. Bush.

Nobody could ever quite fathom where Neil was coming from or where he was going next – certainly not his bandmates. And after the titanic battle of wills between the two alpha males Young and Stills in Buffalo Springfield, you'd have put good money on

ABOVE: Our hero at his most comfortable – with a guitar in his hand and an impassioned song in his heart.

RIGHT: A man with a complex personality.

CHICKEN
DELIGHT

them not being able to coexist in the same time zone, let alone the same working band.

Yet here they were back together again, with the chemistry made more explosive by the presence of another big personality – David Crosby – someone else with an eccentric taste in hats, whose left-wing political rants on stage at the 1967 Monterey Pop Festival led to his dismissal from the Byrds amid accusations of arrogance and dictatorialism. The perfect guy to be in a band with Stephen Stills and Neil Young then.

You actually feared for the sanity of Graham Nash, a thoroughly grounded guy of polite manners and good Northern English stock who applied the commercial ear he'd brought from his old group the Hollies to some of CSNY's biggest hits: "Marrakesh Express", "Our House" and "Teach Your Children" among them.

So, somehow, somewhere, and for some reason, Neil Young got into bed with Crosby, Stills and Nash. "Before I joined I made it clear I belong to myself," he told *Rolling Stone* magazine when they asked what on earth he was thinking, while later he admitted that he enjoyed dipping into people's parties yet cherished the independence that allowed him to dip out again at the drop of a (ludicrously unstylish) hat. That's been Neil's mantra: "I don't want to be in your gang but I'll come and play with your gang until I get bored or find something more exciting to do with my time."

Neil Young perhaps saw potential in Crosby, Stills & Nash to create a monster act, with a rock 'n' roll heart, a Dylan-esque lyrical bite, and a real commercial edge. Or perhaps he couldn't bear to watch the others having a party without him. But mostly, you imagine he genuinely recognized that – despite the recurring

PREVIOUS PAGES: When Crosby, Stills and Nash collaborated with Neil Young, they racked up many hit records, spanning the '60s and '70s.

ABOVE: Photo session for the sleeve of the *Déja Vu* LP. Crosby, Stills, Nash and Young are supplemented by bass player Greg Reeves (sitting, left) and drummer Dallas Taylor (right, with rifle).

tension – when he and Stills were on song they were capable of cooking up something very special.

After Buffalo Springfield split, Stills switched to New York where he hooked up with Jimi Hendrix. He turned down an offer to be lead singer in Blood, Sweat & Tears because he had bigger plans to launch a new all-conquering super band.

Crosby, meanwhile, had been booted out of the Byrds after his own alpha-male confrontation with Roger McGuinn in the middle of recording their *Notorious Byrd Brothers* album, and he went on to produce Joni Mitchell's first album. Graham Nash had quit the Hollies and was hanging out in LA.

Together, Crosby, Stills & Nash created sublime harmonies and some killer songs: soulful, bluesy, a little bit jazzy in places, with sublime harmonies, warmth, complex arrangements, an orgy of instrumentation, and extraordinary attention to detail. Their *Crosby, Stills & Nash* album in 1969 was a runaway success, including the hit singles "Marrakesh Express" (a song Nash had originally written for the Hollies) and "Suite: Judy Blue Eyes". They were creating a very different and identifiable sound that instantly clicked with the public and slotted into the times in which they were living – the album broke the US Top 10 and sold hugely, hanging around in the chart for two years.

Why – you wonder – did the group possibly feel the need to work with the notoriously intense and by now famously truculent Neil Young? They must have known that they ran the risk of scuppering such a runaway success story?

Mostly at the behest of Stills – of all people – the group decided that they needed to beef up their live act and maximize

ABOVE: CSNY in perfect harmony?

OVERLEAF: The CSNY lineup on July 14, 1969.

their tour potential. They needed to deliver their album convincingly onstage, and that was always going to be a problem because it contained so many overdubs that they needed a weighty cavalry to help them out. Lots of big names were bandied around, from the west coast and beyond (Eric Clapton and George Harrison apparently among them) but all were either unavailable or didn't fancy it. And while they debated who they could possibly bring in with sufficient clout to give them the requisite impact on stage, the name Neil Young kept unavoidably floating to the surface.

Having fed off their previous conflicts every bit as avidly as Young had done, Stills was enticed by the suggestion.

Young's star at that point wasn't shining especially brightly. He'd signed a solo deal with Reprise but was disgruntled about the sound quality on his debut album *Neil Young* that hadn't exactly set the world on fire. He'd then taken another turn, setting up his first incarnation of his own band Crazy Horse – a name reflecting a durable fascination with First Nations culture. It was born out of a union with The Rockets (a psychedelic outfit fronted by former doo-wop signer Danny Whitten). They'd met Young some time earlier, and shortly after splitting with Buffalo Springfield, Neil got up on stage and jammed with them at the Whisky-A-Go-Go.

Going into the studio to record a new album, Neil decided to enlist Whitten, Billy Talbot and Ralph Molina from The Rockets as his backup band, rechristening the unified outfit Crazy Horse for their first album *Everybody Knows This Is Nowhere*. It sold respectably enough without pulling up any trees, and assumed its own place in the long list of West Coast albums by now so impressively sculpting the rock landscape. Moulding Crazy Horse into his own image allowed Young to express his more indulgent rock excesses and the album included one of his most ambitious

LEFT: The Thinker.

ABOVE: Duelling egos – Stills and Young trade licks.

efforts from the period – "Down By The River" – a blazing nine-minute guitar blitz built around the slightly discomforting chorus line: "I shot my baby". Neil Young's reputation for "trancing out" on guitar was forged there and then on that one track.

Young was well regarded within the industry and people liked what he was doing with Crazy Horse, but in the commercial terms of CSN, he was *nowhere*.

So for Neil, a place in the front line with Crosby, Stills and Nash made perfect career and profile sense. There was obvious kudos to be drawn from being involved with the biggest band of the moment while gaining overnight a huge audience of his own to be plundered at a later date. The positive ramifications of walking into an established supergroup were too big to ignore. It was win, win, win for Neil.

And yet, "the stubborn one" still dug his heels in when it came to cutting the deal. The original CSN plan was to bring in additional musicians simply as touring musicians – in essence, a backing band – while the proven dollar-making CSN brand continued gloriously unabated. They wanted Neil's input but they didn't want him to be an equal member of the band. They had a name, a reputation, and a golden formula, and after a multi-platinum hit album it made no sense to change it.

But the ways of rock 'n' roll are strange, and album sales don't necessarily possess the same allure as seeing your name up in lights. Neil now had the formidable Elliot Roberts in his corner as manager. Neil knew his worth, and Roberts wasn't going to shrink away from getting his man his due. Neil would buy into the deal if – and *only* if – "and Young" was tagged onto the Crosby, Stills, Nash billing.

The others weren't sure about this at all. Why meddle with a winning formula? But Young and Roberts held firm: no name on the tin; no deal; simple as that. There was to be no compromise.

In the end, of course, the other three caved in. Young's will of iron couldn't be dented – if they wanted him badly enough they had to let him in on his terms. Faced with such unshakeable self-belief, CSN decided that they *did* need him badly enough and let Neil dictate the deal, which included an agreement he would continue with his other band, Crazy Horse.

After the massive success of their first album, all the cards were in the hands of the three original members, but what Neil Young wants, Neil Young usually gets. And so, Crosby, Stills & Nash became Crosby, Stills, Nash & Young.

CSNY were to create moments of blinding inspiration, mixed with episodes of sterility. Stills and Young reconstructed much of their old Buffalo Springfield chemistry, along with the personal

ABOVE: It didn't take long before Neil got bored with the CSNY trip.

RIGHT: Magic in his fingers and iron in his will.

politics that went with it. For all that Young tried to impose his own will on the group, he couldn't get a grip on Nash's commercial sound. The sweet, close-harmony style already closely connected to the band was an uneasy fit for him.

Naturally, it was ego-central in there, too. Nash may well have been forging the core of the group, but Young, Crosby and Stills all appeared to have their own agendas, their own axes to grind, and their own future careers at the forefront of their minds, and, before long, the forces clashed viciously as they fought to be heard. Within weeks they were at each other's throats.

They looked a strange bunch too, even by the weird and wonderful standards of fashion at the time: out-of-control sideburns, impossibly shaggy hair, mad hats, crazy glasses, loon pants and inappropriate vests. The end of the sixties were mad times.

Crosby, Stills & Nash went through a period when they favoured those ridiculously big and heavy greatcoats that looked like they weighed a ton and must have seriously restricted any sort of movement onstage. Not Neil, of course – he always did his own thing. He was a checked shirt, ripped-jeans man to the core who always stood out from the crowd. Or, sometimes during this period, he wore a suit! What a treat that was for the fans. The rest of the band were serious, but Neil Young was *deadly* serious.

A review in the long-defunct *Disc & Music Echo* magazine of one of CSNYs 1969 gigs discussed the dynamic between the members… "They didn't stand up there aloof in their coolness; they made corny jokes, looked awkward and sincere and were obviously having a wonderful time. Graham Nash kept making tea and bad puns. David was too proud and happy to even make more than a feeble political diatribe and Stephen managed to keep his 'aww shucks' humility within reasonable bounds. Neil was Neil. Which is more than good enough, always."

Sounds like they'd had a drink…

Yet, once the band stepped offstage at Woodstock, CSNY were a monster; their name bandied around as a genuine rival to The Beatles in terms of appeal and importance, like a cultural phenomenon. The bandwagon rolled on with the release of *Déjà Vu*, the first album by the four-piece line-up in March, 1970.

Déjà Vu was a colossus. It topped the US charts and produced three major hits, none of them written by Young. Graham Nash wrote "Teach Your Children" and "Our Town", but the biggest of the lot was their cover of Joni Mitchell's poetic reflection on the massive event which had catapulted them to national-institution status the previous year – "Woodstock".

Déjà Vu sold well over two million copies and remains roundly regarded as a classic, but Young appears to have invested little involvement in it. He was a no-show for many of the recording sessions when the other three strove endlessly for barrier-busting perfection, tinkering with overlays, and fine-tuning. Neil disappeared for long periods, and didn't even play on several of the tracks during the elongated recording sessions, which Stills once recklessly estimated to have taken 800 hours of studio time.

It took up a year of CSN's lives, but Neil just wasn't committed enough to put that sort of effort in, especially when he thought it was pointless and preferred to work on his own music rather than engage in the songs of the others. In the end, *Déjà Vu* had just one Young co-write with Stills, called "Everybody I Love You". Young also contributed two songs of his own: "Country Girl", and the achingly raw ballad (which would be hailed as one of his classics) "Helpless".

Neil's dispassionate and dislocated attitude towards the rest of the band meant that he didn't involve them on his own tracks. He did all the overdubs himself on "Country Girl", and treated the hopelessly beautiful "Helpless" as a solo track, with John Sebastian draughted in to play mournful harmonica.

The more *Déjà Vu* sold the more it destroyed the band. Egos went into overload, the drug intake went through the roof, and the accumulation of riches escalated along with all of the bad feeling that goes with it, as three of the four individuals became enveloped by the debilitating onslaught of fame. They bought fast cars, took serious drugs and argued endlessly, regularly squaring up to one another in drunken confrontations on the road. There was a prima donna element, too, with excessive demands in the rider, including a Persian carpet on stage that had to be positioned in exactly the right spot, or there would be hell to pay.

The stage equipment became increasingly more convoluted, the demands grew more ludicrous, the rock 'n' roll excesses hit danger levels, everything went haywire, and the band were wrecked by self-indulgence. At one point, Young stormed offstage during a show in Dallas, after confusingly shouting "if I have to work with Stephen, then Dallas has to go."

They endured emotional traumas too. David Crosby was inconsolable after the death of his girlfriend Christine – the inspiration of one of his best songs, "Guinnevere" – in a car crash; Graham Nash went through a painful split with Joni Mitchell; and Stephen Stills went into emotional meltdown while breaking up with Judy Collins.

PREVIOUS PAGES: Despite their personality clashes, Stephen Sills, Graham Nash, Dallas Taylor, David Crosby, Greg Reeves, and Neil Young had an aura of greatness about them.

RIGHT: Young and son backstage at a CSNY gig.

CSN&

WELMAR

The fans still loved them, of course, grooving happily to the acoustic section of their shows, enjoying Neil's solo bits, dancing around and shaking their heads wildly when the group moved into electric mode.

Inevitably rumours of the band's impending split began almost as soon as Young joined them – not surprising given his total disregard for the conventional band structure, and the well-publicized arguments that followed. By the summer of 1970, dates were being cancelled on a regular basis, with spurious excuses offered. Young's onstage demeanour became increasingly sulky; the audiences got so animated there were real fears shows might escalate into full-scale riots; and members of the backing band, like bass player Greg Reeves and drummer Dallas Taylor, were summarily dismissed after bust-ups. Reeves was evidently sacked by Crosby after a major row when he tried to get one of his own songs included in the set; Taylor because he was debilitated by drug problems.

"How Long Can CSNY Survive?" asked *Melody Maker* magazine in the summer of 1970. "Most of the press corps are holding their breath that the group will stay together to honour their Atlantic contract which calls for one more joint album. However, a spokesman for the label insists that the entire group will return to the studios to record that infamous album as soon as the tour is completed. He further declares that the group will also honour a commitment to tour at the beginning of next year."

Yes, and there's a pig flying past the window...

In the end, it was Stills who took the gunfire when the rest of the band ganged up on him, and after a particularly ostentatious, chest-beating performance at a gig in Colorado, they voted to sack him.

The band never did get to honour the commitment promised by the Atlantic Records spokesman, their contractual obligations fulfilled by the live double LP *4-Way Street* released the following year, taken from shows in New York, Chicago and LA. It confirmed their huge appeal, heading straight to the top of the US charts, but they'd long since disintegrated by then.

Neil Young, of course, had been a detached presence during his entire time with the band. Having already shunned impending celebrity status in several of his earlier songs, he'd long since disassociated himself from the fame game that had consumed the others. He kept himself to himself during the madness,

LEFT: Catching Neil Young smiling was becoming a serious rarity.

ABOVE: How long can CSNY survive?" asked *Melody Maker*. It wasn't long.

maintaining his independence and juggling the demands of CSNY with the other things around him that were closer to his heart, like the ongoing Crazy Horse.

Nobody could understand why he'd want to spend time, energy and talent on what was a relatively minor success, at the same time as he was a full-on member of one of the world's biggest bands. But that, in a nutshell, explains the curious psyche of Young. He was never like other rock stars. This was a guy deeply uneasy if he ever found he was in step with the crowd.

While the others were partying, parading and strutting their stuff, Young had bigger fish to fry. Awash with ideas and a million unwritten songs in his head, Neil was never going to be contained in an outfit where he had to compete so vigorously for space with three other strong talents and big personalities, where fame and self-aggrandizement were so evidently constricting creativity. So, at the same time as he was locking horns with Stills and the others in CSNY, he was trying to record a new album with Crazy Horse.

In his long career of ever-changing moods and contradictory shifts of stance and style, Crazy Horse is the nearest Neil has come to a constant – a band much closer to his heart than CSNY ever were. He may have destroyed a perfectly good band The Rockets in pilfering them for his own purposes, but their own relative lack of success in various forays without Neil suggests they needed him more than he needed them, whatever Jack Nitzsche and Nils Lofgren may have brought to the party when they joined.

Young seems to have regarded Crazy Horse almost as a safe haven – an escape from the ego meltdowns of CSNY – where he could do his own thing and indulge his passion for grittier music. It was always rough and ready with Crazy Horse, and that's exactly how Neil liked it.

Crazy Horse failed to achieve any great international success mostly because Neil simply didn't want it that way, directing them firmly under the radar, refusing to play record company games and sell themselves in the usual way. It then became an underground cloak that they couldn't shake off even when Neil wasn't around. Crazy Horse recorded fast and live, and they came to be a significant force on several of Young's best albums (as well as his crazier projects) for over four decades. It wasn't all plain sailing though: Crazy Horse were touched by tragedy when their founder Danny Whitten died in 1972.

As a unit and as a brand, Crazy Horse allowed Young to express himself at his own leisure without encountering drama from either the record company or other musicians. Neil dipped in and out of Crazy Horse seemingly at will, often appearing completely ruthless and high-handed in his treatment of them; fully engaging with them one minute, dispensing with their services without warning or explanation the next.

But, having long since abandoned ambitions of making it on their own, Crazy Horse have been loyal to Neil, and in his own way Neil has been loyal back, returning time and again to the reliable henchmen who will support even his wildest schemes and put up with his irascible behaviour. Certainly since Crazy Horse settled into a regular, longstanding lineup of Billy Talbot on bass, Ralph Molina on drums and Frank Sampedro on guitar they have grown accustomed to Neil's eccentricities, while he has come to rely on their adaptability. Neil praised their unlimited reserves of energy and strength, and Crazy Horse perhaps aren't the shrinking violets of popular misconception, offering a proactive and decisive contribution to the recording process that makes their union with Young – whenever the call comes – seem completely natural.

Neil could never quite turn his back on CSNY completely, despite the same old problems invariably attached, like when they committed the cardinal sin of live music by doing stadium tours in 1974. Neil travelled alone to the gigs, had his own roadie, studiously avoided the Learjets the rest of the band travelled in, and cast a cynical eye over the proceedings with his lopsided smile, huge shades, patched jeans and stripey jacket far too big for him.

A 1988 reunion resulted in CSNY's second studio LP *American Dream* – a concept album of sorts that showed how disparate they'd all become as individuals – an insipid collection of songs that did none of them any justice. It even made No. 4 in a book called *The Worst Rock & Roll Records Of All Time*.

And then, another decade on, there was another unsatisfactory effort – *Looking Forward* – when Young suddenly decided to mount his white charger and save his old mates as they struggled to rebuild their careers after a period in the doldrums. Against all odds and sensible advice, Neil even went back on the road with them.

The image of Neil Young as a heroic fixer riding to the rescue of his old friends isn't one that sits easily. Except perhaps in his own head. Neil was never born to be a team player, but what he invariably brought to the fold always guaranteed explosive results.

Buffalo Springfield, CSNY and Crazy Horse are talented line-ups that played their parts in rock history, but ultimately they were all about Neil Young. He wouldn't have it any other way...

RIGHT: Backstage with Crosby, Stills, Nash and Young.

CHAPTER 3

TIME FADING AWAY

"WHATEVER DID HAPPEN TO Woodstock Nation?" wrote the esteemed rock critic Nick Kent in 1973 in a brutal review of Neil Young's latest album *Time Fades Away* which essentially dismissed him as a credible force. Arguing that his artistic worth had been in terminal decline since his departure from CSNY, he decided Neil suffered from the "dreaded superstar disease of self-parody" on 1970's *After The Gold Rush* and that the "wimpish" and "tiresome" *Harvest* in 1972 had all the hallmarks of "just another lonely pop star" who'd "lost his credibility in the process".

Harsh stuff, but that was nothing to Kent's vicious dismantling of the live album *Time Fades Away*, on which he announced our hero had hit rock bottom. "Sloppy attempts at rock 'n' roll … tiresome chord progressions … obscure nonsense lyrics … a mess … his voice is more annoying than ever … embarrassing listening … offensive to the ears."

Kent was only just warming up, however, completing his hatchet job with the conclusion that "*Time Fades Away* proves once and for all that, like so many others who get elevated to superstar status, Neil Young has now got nothing to say for himself."

It was a harsh analysis, but in some ways a fair one. Neil himself later described *Time Fades Away* as the worst record he ever made, but Young's music is nothing if not the product of how he views the world, and at the time he was in another dark place. Although "dark" is putting it lightly – he was in a very bad spot indeed. And much of it was to do with Danny Whitten.

LEFT: *Harvest* turned Neil into a household name, but it didn't make him happy.

ABOVE: Crazy Horse circa 1975. Left to right: Ralph Molina, Billy Talbot, Frank Sampedro, Neil Young … and boat.

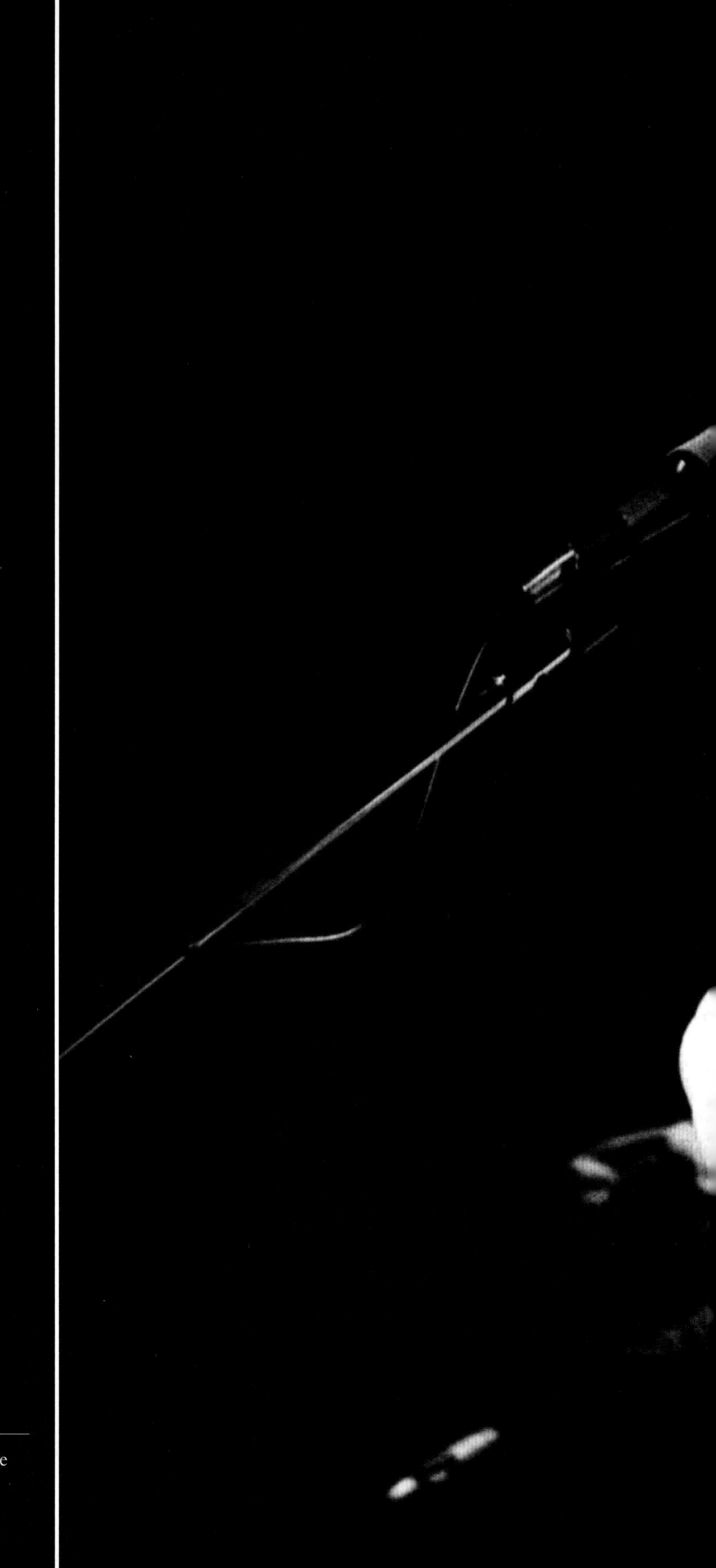

White jacket and dark music – Neil in "Ditch Trilogy" mode around the time of the release of *Tonight's The Night* in 1975.

Alone, Whitten made many attempts to get clean, and when it appeared that he was winning the battle, Young encouraged him back into the fold to work on new material for the *Time Fades Away* tour, from which a live album would be recorded. But it wasn't long before Danny began using again, and a distraught Young fired him for a second time before the tour had got beyond the rehearsal stage.

When Danny died shortly later, Neil was devastated. The tragedy haunted Neil for many years, and he blamed himself for not doing more to help his friend when he needed him most. In the good times, they'd worked intuitively together. Whitten was one of the few musicians with whom Neil formed a natural bond, and the manner of his death formed a black cloud that brooded heavily over Young. The morose *Time Fades Away* was essentially a self-flagellating homage to Danny Whitten.

The day after Whitten's death, Young reputedly sat down to write his most autobiographical song to date, "Don't Be Denied".

PREVIOUS PAGES LEFT: Neil on the Crazy Horse bandwagon in Copenhagen, Denmark, 1976. Neil Young's stylistic influence on Nirvana's Kurt Cobain is plain to see.

PREVIOUS PAGES RIGHT: Neil Young's checked shirts are one of his most iconic fashion statements.

LEFT: Neil sacked Crazy Horse halfway through recording *After The Gold Rush* in 1970, with spectacular results.

The other material he'd already written for the *Time Fades Away* tour suddenly took on a grimmer form and was performed differently. "The bridge was falling down and that took a lot of lies and it made me lonely," he wailed painfully on the "The Bridge", while the caustic "L.A." was reinvested with a doomy, almost demonic intensity. Young seemed to be going out of his way to create a deeply uncomfortable, ugly environment that left listeners on the edge. If an album ever reflected the mood of its creator, then *Time Fades Away* was it, and it's little wonder that Kent and other critics tore it to pieces.

With 62 dates in large stadiums, the *Time Fades Away* album was the biggest project Neil had ever undertaken – but for everyone involved it seemed a whole lot longer. Charmless, confrontational and unapproachable throughout, Young became a simmering ball of misery. The album would change the whole landscape of his career.

Although Nick Kent might not have thought much of Neil Young's latest work, he was out of kilter with majority opinion and public taste, and so *After The Gold Rush* and *Harvest* became two of Neil's most successful albums, both artistically and commercially.

Recorded amid the madness of CSNY, *After The Gold Rush* was a strange hybrid, initially intended as the soundtrack music to a movie that never actually got made. If Young's motive for joining CSNY in the first place had been to boost his personal profile and solo career, then it worked beautifully, as *After The Gold Rush* burst into the Top 10 of the US album charts.

Then Neil's whole public persona changed due to his most successful song to emerge under the CSNY banner – a rare political song that redefined Neil as a man in tune with the thinking of a generation. The song in question revolves around one of the most shameful events in modern American history.

It all started on Monday May 4, 1970, when 2,000 students and supporters at Kent State University in Ohio held a campus protest in response to an announcement by President Nixon that the US would escalate the Vietnam War by invading Cambodia.

Tensions soon mounted: draft cards and copies of the US Constitution were burned, resulting in disturbances throughout the city of Kent. The mayor announced a state of emergency and the National Guard were sent in to root out the troublemakers, using tear gas to restore order against protesters dismissed as communists and revolutionaries.

RIGHT: "That old King was a friend of mine, never knew a dog that was half as fine..." Neil's "Heart Of Gold" hit spearheaded the *Harvest* album to massive sales, and the celebrity status it won him made him reassess his career.

A protest planned on the campus on May 4 was officially banned by university officials but went ahead anyway, and the National Guard were greeted with a volley of rocks when they arrived to disperse the protesters. High winds meant that the National Guard's tear gas was useless and suddenly the guardsmen pulled out their weapons and started shooting, seemingly indiscriminately.

In the carnage that followed, four students aged between 19 and 20 died – two of whom weren't even involved in the protest – and nine others were injured.

Lots of claims and counterclaims followed about who was to blame for the tragedy, but it quickly became an open sore for America. Galvanized students right across the country rose up against the Nixon administration and attitudes hardened against the war. America's great moral majority, however, placed the blame squarely on the students, driving an even bigger wedge into a generation gap dividing the good citizens of the USA from an angry new youth culture.

Music, naturally, fed into the mood of the time, and there was no shortage of songwriters dashing out songs emotively condemning Nixon, the National Guard, the student authorities and others caught up in the political fall-out … Steve Miller's "Jackson-Kent Blues", the Beach Boys' "Student Demonstration Time", Bruce Springsteen's "Where Was Jesus In Ohio?", Harvey

ABOVE: "Hell I don't know!" – Neil's response to Dolly Parton, when she phoned him to ask what "After The Gold Rush" was about.

RIGHT: Is that a smile or a grimace? Neil Young in San Francisco, performing at the Winterland arena circa 1973.

Gibson

Andrews' "Hey Sandy", Barbara Dane's "Kent State Massacre", and Holly Near's "It Could Have Been Me".

But the highest profile of them all was Neil Young's "Ohio".

"Tin soldiers and Nixon coming, we're finally on our own. This summer I hear the drumming, four dead in Ohio," sang Young, tuning into the mood of distress, fury and rebellion now occupying the younger strand of American culture.

Yet Young didn't write "Ohio" as a career move (has he ever done *anything* as a career move?) It was simply his instant, emotional response to harrowing photographs of the disaster he saw in *Life* magazine, and those who heard him play it for the first time instantly knew he'd come up with something that would resonate with a whole generation. "It was probably the biggest lesson ever learned at an American place of learning," Neil wrote in his liner notes for the *Decade* collection.

"Ohio" was recorded quickly, too, and released as a CSNY single, passing their other hit song "Teach Your Children" on the way up to No. 14 in the US singles charts, capturing one of the few truly harmonious moments in CSNY's existence. Young later commented that he thought it was the best thing CSNY ever recorded – a song that defined music in a different way for him – a real statement which had a genuinely unifying effect on the attitudes of a particular strand of society.

Through Woody Guthrie, Bob Dylan and many others, people have argued for decades about whether music has the power to change things or alter society's perceptions of events. Possibly not, but a song like "Ohio" definitely has the strength to consolidate, inspire and unite opinion – and it *did*. It even got banned on AM Radio stations due to its references to Nixon – surely its biggest accolade of all – although there have been some stonking cover versions down the years too – notably from Paul Weller, Mott the Hoople, Devo, and The Dandy Warhols.

"Ohio", and the enthusiastic response it generated as a heavyweight slab of social commentary, was a major landmark for Young, and lent great impetus to the subsequent *After The Gold Rush*; an album that looked like becoming a complete shambles, as Danny Whitten's descent into drugs hell began to run out of control. Young himself was evolving fast as a writer, and in the end the album turned out to be a very different beast to the raucous rocker he'd originally intended, which was essentially the hard and fast style he'd trailblazed on *Everybody Knows This Is Nowhere* 15 months earlier. This was an antidote to the smooth indulgence of CSNY, and the plan was for *After The Gold Rush* to be a reaction against the whole CSNY ethos of pop melodies and production overload. Instead, the planned antithesis of commercial thinking led to the most lucrative period in Neil's career.

Young wrote another rare political song, "Southern Man", which exposed a painful sore in American social history – racism and bigotry in the south. Reputedly inspired by an incident encountered on a tour in the south with Buffalo Springfield when a bunch of rednecks took exception to the invasion of the long-haired reprobates and tried to chase them out of town, the raging "Southern Man" caused quite a stir. "Southern change gonna come at last, now your crosses are burning fast..." Neil roared, suddenly in the realms of a bona fide protest song.

It's a topic Young came to pursue even more bitterly on "Alabama" from his next album *Harvest*, inciting southern boogie band Lynryd Skynryd to write their own song "Sweet Home Alabama" in response, even giving Young a dismissive namecheck in their own lyrics. Years later, Young himself seemed embarrassed by both songs, saying he'd much rather hear Lynyrd Skynyrd's than his own.

And yet, despite the brutal nature of "Southern Man", there's an engaging accessibility about it as well, which opened the door to the unexpected onrush of commercial success. No small credit for this dramatic turn of events should go to Mr. Nils Lofgren. Half-Swedish and half-Italian – Chicago-born Lofgren was 17 when he first talked his way backstage at the Cellar Door club, Washington DC, and played Young some of his songs.

The story of Lofgren's involvement with Neil and the impact he made in the shifting direction of *After The Gold Rush* says much about the unconventional approach of Young and his conviction that rock music *should* be edgy and impure and not produced to within an inch of its life.

"A strange and wondrous adventure" is how Lofgren later described his time with Young, and you can only imagine his shock and delight that a member of one of the biggest bands in the world had singled him out, taken him under his wing, helped get his band Grin a record deal, and asked him to play on his solo album. Always big on the risk factor, with a dislike of the comfort zone, Neil decided that the young guitarist should also play piano on the album.

What he saw in Lofgren was the open mind of a musician well versed in classical, jazz and big band music, and, fuelled on confidence and self-belief, someone well qualified to bring a different feel to an instrument he'd scarcely played before. Nils had tinkered with accordion a bit, but playing piano in a rock band was something different entirely. "Basic" is the word Lofgren later used

PREVIOUS PAGES: Behind closed doors – here in rehearsal and not aware of the picture being taken – Neil Young was more relaxed.

LEFT: Neil moved into another realm when he reacted to the Kent State University students massacre with the protest song "Ohio".

to describe his playing on *After The Gold Rush* while Young called him the "classic barrel-roll piano player". Clearly it worked for both of them.

Whether by design or accident, Lofgren's playing had a key role in the mellow vibe of *After The Gold Rush*, a vibe elegantly demonstrated by the dreamy eponymous track that was to take on a life of its own, cutting across all genres. British trio Prelude sang it unaccompanied and took it into charts all over the world, and its innate, mysterious beauty seduced plenty of others along the way too – Flamin' Lips, Tori Amos, Thom Yorke, et al. – even if they didn't have a clue what the song was about. Knights in armour? Peasants singing and drummers drumming? Mother nature on the run? Burned-out basements? Silver spaceships? Children crying?

Was this Neil Young ruminating on the apocalypse or was he just away with the fairies when he wrote "After the Gold Rush"? Dylanesque degrees of analysis have gone into deciphering every oblique reference, and people have described the song as everything from a drug anthem, to a damning indictment of the failings of ecology, to a personal vision of mortality; but nobody who played this game ever got any concrete answers. Not even Dolly Parton, who told a lovely story about being so desperate to know the background to the song when she recorded it with Emmylou Harris and Linda Ronstadt that she got Young's number and called him up to ask what it was about. "Hell, I don't know, I just *wrote* it,' replied Neil, "it just depends on what I was taking at the time…"

Nothing, however, screws a serious artist up quite like a hit single – a proper hit single. "Ohio" was a hit, of course, but was still very much an alternative song that flew in the face of the establishment (just how Neil liked it). *Heart Of Gold* was something else though. A No. 1 single – his *only* No 1 single – it

LEFT: On fire – Neil Young blows away an audience on Guy Fawkes Night (November 5) at The Rainbow Theatre in London, 1973.

ABOVE: Hit singles? Huge-selling albums? It felt like the Apocalypse for Neil Young.

was pretty enough, unthreatening enough and sentimental enough to catapult him right into the heart of the establishment.

The album – *Harvest* – from where the aforementioned singles came, topped both the US and the UK charts to propel Neil Young to a new plateau. Fame, acceptance, acclaim – he had it all – achieving a level of commercial popularity even greater than CSNY. Neil Young could never be content with all *that*, and the runaway success of "Heart Of Gold" inevitably left him questioning the ethics of mass popularity – specifically his own role in it – eliciting from him a famous quote about the song putting him "in the middle of the road" and triggering a sharp change of direction into less inviting terrain. "Travelling there soon became a bore so I headed for a ditch – a rougher ride, but I met more interesting people there," he said.

Just because "Heart Of Gold" was soothing and the whole *Harvest* album was reflective, it didn't mean the turbulence of CSNY had ceased. There was the breakup of Neil's marriage to Susan Acevedo – the one person who found celebrity even more distasteful than Neil himself – and a new relationship with actress Carrie Snodgress.

The *Harvest* sessions were also blighted by Neil's chronic back problems which severely restricted his electric guitar playing. The enforced sedentary recovery period from a disc operation contributed to the overriding laidback nature of the album. Everything was enhanced by several tracks recorded in Nashville with local musicians who became dubbed the Stray Gators. These songs, like "Are You Ready For The Country" and "Old Man", had a lonesome tinge. Bathed in banjo and pedal steel guitar, with James Taylor and Linda Ronstadt on backing vocals, "Old Man" was widely assumed to have been written about Neil's dad – not least by Mr. Young Sr. – but was actually written for Louis Avila, a cattleman and caretaker of the ranch Neil had bought in Northern California from the first flush of his accumulating wealth.

Harvest also includes one of Neil's most hauntingly personal songs, "The Needle & The Damage Done", that is dripping with despair stemming from the habits of Danny Whitten, who was still alive at the time but slithering into a distressing decline. "I sing the song because I love the man. I know that some of you don't understand…" sang Young, partly inspired by "Needle Of Death" by one of his early heroes Bert Jansch.

ABOVE: Trusty banjo and trustier shirt: Young rediscovers his country soul.

RIGHT: Never try to separate a rock star from his shades.

ABOVE: Young in presidential pose.

ABOVE RIGHT: In conference with Van Morrison and Joni Mitchell, California, 1976.

RIGHT: There was something myesterious about those eyes – what was going on behind them?

OPPOSITE: Demonstrating dance steps with Billy Talbot.

There were no shortage of accusations of "sellout", and the softer side to *Harvest* certainly had many rock fans writing Neil off, assuming it was the catalyst for him to go the way of so many others seduced by mainstream success who settle for cosy middle ground. "I happened to be in the right place at the right time to do a really mellow record that was really open because that's where my life was at the time," Neil said. "I thought the record was good. But I knew something else was dying..."

What was dying was Neil's rock 'n' roll soul and he wanted it back. So he very consciously and deliberately started shattering his mainstream persona with the deeply inaccessible *Time Fades Away*. It was self-sabotage, plain and simple, and it worked perfectly. *Time Fades Away* (and indeed the disjointed soundtrack for his documentary movie about his career so far *Journey Through The Past*) bombed and Neil was a superstar no more.

Having turned his back on the bland commercial opportunities offered so fulsomely by "Heart of Gold" and *Harvest*, Young's career might easily have perished in a splurge of wilful neglect. He certainly took no prisoners in the mid-1970s. *Tonight's The Night* glowered and scowled at you in an intimidating manner – a bleak, crude and overtly heavy response to the deaths of Danny Whitten and, the following year, Young's roadie Bruce Berry, that sounded so darkly vicious, Reprise didn't even want to release it at all.

Before releasing this album, Young filled in the time perfecting it by releasing the marginally less pessimistic *On The Beach* that contained references to cult leader and mass murderer Charles Manson who Young had actually met (on the song "Revolution Blues"), Richard Nixon and kidnapped heiress Patty Hearst ("Ambulance Blues"), oil barons ("Vampire Blues"), and his partner Carrie Snodgress ("Motion Pictures").

Neither album sent the cash tills ringing; not surprising given the harsh, unrelenting nature of the content, which didn't as much shift Neil away from the middle of the road as it did launch several grenades into it. Three guerrilla albums – the so-called "Ditch Trilogy" – and the soft centred, melodic, country-style of "Heart Of Gold" was gone forever along with (many thought) Neil's career...

ABOVE, ABOVE RIGHT: If you want to get on Neil Young's good side, just talk to him about vintage cars...

Strange messages popped up in the liner notes to *Tonight's The Night* to perpetuate the myth that Neil had lost his marbles. "I'm sorry. You don't know these people. This means nothing to you," randomly appears on the sleeve without explanation, while the insert includes a letter to "Waterface". Asked to explain the reference by his biographer Jimmy McDonough, Young says that the mysterious Waterface is himself, and the letter is "a suicide note without the suicide". The insert also included a review written in Dutch and the lyrics to a song "Florida" that wasn't actually included on the LP at all.

It's little wonder that Neil's record company, other associates, critics and fans despaired of him. *Rolling Stone* magazine, for example, described *On The Beach* as "one of the most despairing albums of the decade". In his review in *Creem* magazine, Wayne Robins described *Tonight's The Night* as "so dark, so personal, so filled with needles that go bump in the night, that one can only wonder how long Neil Young could survive if he didn't have a time warp to give his natural life a little distance from the real blade that he insists on teasing against his own throat."

"I don't even think I'm in the record business anymore," Young told *Creem* in 1975, while uncharacteristically doing some promotion work for an album in which he held genuine conviction. "It's not a friendly album but it's real," he said, confirming it had achieved its intention to be a sharp kick in the groin of the whole superstar circus, shattering any lingering remnants of his *Harvest* persona as a smooth balladeer. "We gotta tear down all that – it's gone now," he said. "Now we can do whatever. It's open again, there's no illusions that someone can say what I'm going to do before I get there … if that's the way it is, then I quit."

It's not fair to state that a particular decade defined Neil Young, because the man has spent his entire career avoiding definition, but the 1970s comprehensively solidified Neil's self-image as an anti-star. He spent the first part of the decade rocketing to superstardom both with CSNY and with his own solo work. He then spent the middle of that decade routinely dismantling his legacy, angrily rejecting almost everything that most other musicians and the record industry held so dear.

By the end of the decade, though, Neil had fully reasserted himself, and those he'd left behind cottoned onto the logic of his independence. Neil proved it was possible to turn your back on all the bullshit that accompanies fame and popularity, withstand the rejection and ridicule that follows, survive the misunderstanding and scorn of critics and the dismay and disillusionment of fans … and come back fighting. Neil Young bit the hand that fed him and lived to tell the tale.

Young's high-risk policy certainly earned him the respect of his peers – at least the peers he cared about – underlined by his appearance on stage alongside Bob Dylan, Joni Mitchell, Van Morrison and many other groovier rock acts of the day at *The Last Waltz* – the high-profile farewell performance of The Band in San Francisco. Unlike Woodstock, Young agreed to be filmed in Martin Scorsese's movie of the event, even if Scorsese may have preferred otherwise when he was asked to re-edit the film so that viewers wouldn't be able to see the cocaine wedged up his nose.

In truth *The Last Waltz* was a bit of a shambles. The film was universally panned and an exhausted, overwrought Young struggled to get through his set, which included a painful performance of "Helpless" with The Band. And yet the publicity did him no harm at all.

Despite the collapse of his relationship with Carrie Snodgress, referenced in the seven-minute "Danger Bird", the 1975 album *Zuma* signaled an emergence from the darkness of the "Ditch Trilogy" and, astonishingly, a reunion with Stephen Stills to release *Long May You Run* as the Stills-Young band, with predictable results. The group survived just nine days on the road together when Stills received a telegram from Young containing the words "Dear Stephen. Funny how some things that start spontaneously end that way. Eat a peach. Neil."

New albums were started, dumped, rejigged and then dumped again, but 1977's *American Stars 'n' Bars* met some of his old fans halfway with its country-rock slant and a barroom ambience which Young self-parodyingly said captured his lifestyle at the time: "You know, drunk on my ass in bars." It was hardly one of his greatest works, yet the album did include one of his most epic and durable songs, the hypnotic "Like A Hurricane" – a fireball of frenzied guitar and bass.

Neither *American Stars 'n' Bars* nor its successor *Comes A Time* can seriously claim to sit among the upper echelons of Young's vast canon of work, but right at the end of the decade, his regeneration rocketed with the unlikely catalyst of the punk revolution. Punk had arisen to overthrow the rock dinosaurs – like CSNY – and, having tried for most of the decade to do the same thing in terms of his own career, Young approved heartily.

Neil put a new band together who turned up to play unannounced in small bars as The Ducks, and befriended alternative

ABOVE: The master of melancholy lightens up.

RIGHT: Neil builds up to trademark stage frenzy.

punk band Devo. One of the songs Neil sang with the Ducks "My My, Hey Hey (Out Of The Blue)" became a cause célèbre. Apart from its line "it's better to burn out than to fade away" that was immortalized in Kurt Cobain's suicide note, it included another telling couplet that resonated around the world: "The king is gone but he's not forgotten. This is the story of a Johnny Rotten."

Suitably energized, Neil included two versions of the song – one electric, one acoustic – on the album *Rust Never Sleeps* whose title reputedly was suggested by Devo, who covered "My My, Hey Hey". The project closed out the decade, and put Neil slap-bang right back in the centre of public consciousness and social thinking.

Neil was roaring again. Capturing the full thrust of Young's vehement stage show, *Rust Never Sleeps* was voted the best album in 1979's *Rolling Stone* Critics' Poll, comprehensively restoring both his commercial viability and his artistic credibility. *Harvest* and "Heart Of Gold" were suddenly but a distant memory.

Even Nick Kent, the critic who'd dismissed Neil as a dinosaur a few years earlier, ate his own words: "Very simply *Rust* is the finest album Neil Young has ever released," he stated boldly. "The ever intrigued Young watcher can at last see a wickedly devious method in what seemed all too often to be a blinkered, idiosyncratic madness … *Rust Never Sleeps* spotlights our hero in complete control of his genius."

In six loaded, eventful years since Kent had written him off, Young had resurrected and reinvented himself in startling fashion.

LEFT: The two sides of Neil were shown when he came back to form on *Rust Never Sleeps* in 1979, partly recorded on stage.

ABOVE: Neil had cause to rue his famous line "it's better to burn out than to fade away".

CHAPTER 4

PRISONER OF ROCK ’N’ ROLL?

Only the very brave or very foolish would contemplate making an enemy of David Geffen. A Brooklyn-born Jew who launched his Geffen label in 1980 with heavyweight acts like Donna Summer and John Lennon, the ruthlessly ambitious Geffen quickly established himself as one of the most formidable and powerful characters in the music industry. He was not a man to suffer fools or dissenters gladly; not a man to be trifled with.

Then again, Neil Young isn't too fussy who he trifles with…

The immovable object met the original force when Young's long relationship with Reprise Records hit rock bottom in the wake of his continuing desire to experiment and confound, confusing everyone else in the process.

Neil had issues to deal with, lots of issues, many of them centred on his severely handicapped son Ben who, like his half-brother Zeke, had been diagnosed with cerebral palsy. The near-death of Neil's wife Pegi from a brain tumour also distracted him from music and, with his mind and priorities elsewhere, he was off the road for an extended period, and his career and profile suffered as a result.

The records Neil did make explored tangents that didn't rest well with the public. There was the vaguely political *Hawks & Doves*, an untidy mix of old (some of them dating back to 1974) and new recordings with a strong country bias that Neil tried to shape into a puzzling concept about the threat of the Cold War and the advent of Reaganism to avert it.

Here is a guy who became a darling of the left by taking on Nixon and damning the Kent State University massacres on "Ohio"; who invoked the wrath of the good ol' boys in the south by confronting racist history on "Southern Man" and "Alabama"; and who – just by his stubborn antipathy towards the trite values of the big, bad record industry – had a social heart that was fully in tune with the folk-music community that had partly spawned him.

Suddenly Neil was singing "I ain't tongue-tied, just don't got nothin' to say. I'm proud to be livin' in the USA…" on *Hawks and Doves*, and nobody quite knew what he was about any more. He seemed to be speaking for America's great silent majority. He seemed to be issuing an unequivocal rallying cry for patriotism. He seemed to be nailing his colours firmly to the mast of Ronald Reagan – America's most right-wing president for years. "Ready to go, willing to stay and pay, so my sweet love can dance another free day. USA … USA…" he sang, and then, almost jingoistically, finished with, "If you hate us, you just don't know what you're sayin'."

Neil even went in for a bit of union bashing – specifically the Musician Union's "Keep Music Live" campaign on the sardonic "Union Man". Middle American themes of family values were reaffirmed in the simplistic assertion of loyalty in "Stayin' Power", which was a clear personal recognition of Neil's own sense of duty to his wife and disabled child.

Yet if all this suggested Neil had unaccountably turned into a flag-waving conservative, then "Coming Apart At Every Nail" comprehensively contradicted this view, with couplets like "Hey hey, ain't that right, the working man's in a hell of a fight"; "this country sure looks good to me, but these fences are coming apart at every nail" and "meanwhile at the Pentagon, the brass was a-wondering what went wrong."

Hawks and Doves was released the very same day Ronald Reagan was elected as US president. It was the work of a born-again reactionary at a time when Americans were becoming a target for hostage takers in Iran. Was it a cunningly disguised satire on America's ballooning suspicion of Russia and extreme patriotism?

This album was part of what makes Young such a durably fascinating subject. He's a closed book hiding behind a myriad of bewildering cloaks and ambiguity. "I walk a fine line," Young admitted to writer Bill Flanagan a few years later. "There is a character in there but he reflects a lot of the ways I have felt. I can say things through somebody else that I couldn't say myself."

Pushed by Flanagan on his political outlook at the time, he agreed he supported Reagan – "a good man and a good leader" – while expressing his pride in the USA, despite the fact that as a Canadian he's not allowed to vote anyway. "I'm proud to be living in the United States, I'm proud of what this country is doing. I've been all over the world and I feel at home here."

None of which propelled him into the arms of the right wing or made *Hawks and Doves* much of a seller. Less still its follow-up, *Re-ac-tor*, with its flailing barrage of electric guitars, overdubs and sound effects guaranteed to frighten off any republicans wearing the Stars and Stripes.

The patience of Neil's record company Reprise was tested to the limit by the relatively poor performances of the two albums, as Young continued to avoid promotion and dodge the sort of material that made him so successful in the first place: "Looking the devil in the eye," as he put it. "I hate being labelled, I hate to be stuck in one thing. I just don't want to be anything for very long. I just want to keep moving, keep running, play my guitar…"

And if Reprise was dismayed by Neil's persistent rejections of all conventional commercial practices, it would have looked with disapproval at one track in particular on the *Re-ac-tor* album called "Surfer Jo and Mo The Sleaze", a Dylanesque title parodying the music industry, with two top Reprise executives the apparent target.

Right: A man who loves to confront and confound … especially when it comes to politics.

Add to this one of the most impenetrable tracks he'd ever recorded – the nine-minute "T-Bone" – an improvisational, irritatingly repetitive assault, and *Re-ac-tor* was an album with few saving graces.

Except, perhaps, the intense closing track, "Shots", which featured Young playing with his new toy, the Synclavier digital synthesizer, which showed the first signs of leading him in another direction entirely that would make *Re-ac-tor* seem like a bubblegum record.

As tensions mounted and sales faltered, Reprise wearied of Neil's unpredictability, while Neil in turn felt that the label didn't believe in him and just wasn't backing him in the way he deserved. As relations broke down, their 13-year, seven-album association was stretched to the breaking point. Deeply involved in a new programme to help handicapped children, Neil shut off the lines of communication and showed little interest in building bridges or trying to rescue the situation.

RCA steamed in with a lucrative contract offer, but was cut off at the pass by the looming, somewhat intimidating figure of David Geffen, who saw Young as the ideal, credible candidate to get his fledgeling label up and running. He offered Neil a five-album deal at $1m an album, and – more crucially as far as Neil was concerned – complete artistic freedom.

"David totally relates to Neil as an artist and he has no preconceived notions ... he knows he's capable of doing anything at any point at any time," Neil's manager Elliot Roberts told the Young fanzine *Broken Arrow* with some prescience when the deal was cut. Oh, how those words would come back to haunt him...

Geffen and Roberts had worked together closely and harmoniously in the CSNY days and Young had no hesitation in signing up to Geffen's vision. It was a decision he soon came to bitterly regret.

Disappearing to Hawaii to make a mellow, acoustic record that he wanted to call *Island In The Sun*, Neil soon discovered that "total artistic freedom" only worked if Geffen liked what he heard. Geffen went to Hawaii and *didn't* like what he heard.

Neil – by now a big fan of Kraftwerk and the oblique potential of the electro-pop era sweeping Europe – took Geffen's criticism to heart, and turned instead to his Synclavier and the wonder of gadgets. The end result was *Trans*, probably the most extreme, left field, bizarre and riskiest album in a career dripping with such beasts.

Released at the end of 1982, *Trans* was essentially an album of computer music which at times sounded almost inhuman, Neil's disembodied vocals contorted by excessive use of a vocoder. "With the new digital and computerized equipment now I can do things I could never do before," he said proudly. Which was true enough, but whether this was something anyone else would want to hear him doing is a matter that fiercely divided Young watchers. "If you don't experiment you're dead," he added defiantly.

Neil's words cut no ice with the critics, who gave him the biggest kicking of his career for the album (including his old adversary Nick Kent, who was back on the attack again, describing it as "an unintelligible sci-fi rock opera about computers that made no sense to anyone.")

They pilloried the incomprehensible lyrics, the overload of technology, the coldness of the production, the aimlessness of the tunes, and the listlessness of it all. Not an idea, not a note, not a song, was spared the wrath and ridicule of the critics who even accused Neil of wrecking one of his own best songs on his harsh and dispassionate remake of Buffalo Springfield's "Mr. Soul".

Young would argue the album's worth, explaining the methodology of exploring the exciting new potential offered by electronic equipment as a means of expressing his own very personal recent experiences in finding a way to communicate with his disabled son, Ben, who had no power of speech. "At that time he was simply trying to find a way to communicate with other people," said Neil. "That's what *Trans* is all about. On that record you know I'm saying something, but you don't know what it is. Well, that's exactly the same feeling I was getting from my son."

This is persuasive background information, but it didn't convince critics, fans or his new record boss, and the album bombed badly at the cash tills. But is *Trans* as bad as everyone perceived at the time? Is it Neil's equivalent of *Metal Machine Music* and John Lennon's *Two Virgins*, or is it – as Young himself almost pleadingly contests – just woefully misunderstood; an album so far ahead of its time that it flew over people's heads?

Listening to it now it still jars, but while he'd constantly reinvented his music up until that time, *Trans* surely represents a different way of listening, not just to Neil Young, but to rock music generally. It's music that's all about spirit, atmosphere, mood and mental imagery – a radical departure from the more literal way we are used to hearing music that is dependent on notes, lyrics and tone. It certainly sounds unreal, but within the bombardment of effects and messed-up vocals, a sense of reason does crawl out if you let it, particularly if you're armed with the knowledge about a stricken son unable to talk or communicate. Even Young's robotic reimagining of "Mr. Soul" is light years away from its Stones-fuelled origins and carries with it a compelling emotional power that bears little resemblance to the original version.

In the 1980s, Neil became engaged in the great Artistic Freedom Wars with David Geffen.

Lost in the moment – Neil Young trances out onstage in Paris, 1983.

The biggest argument against *Trans* – and about electronic music generally – is that it is cold, unemotional and impersonal. Listen with open ears and that's simply not the case with *Trans*, a subliminal powerhouse on which can also be found one of his finest songs, "Transformer Man" – his most direct reference to his son's harrowing physical state – it's full of love, anguish and pathos.

Trans is a painfully soul-bearing work – Young describes it as his most personal album – and it must have taken a great deal for this intensely private man to share his reaction to a brutal family experience with the world through his music, however obliquely he chose to shroud it in technology behind synthesizers and vocoders.

It would be futile to argue that *Trans* is one of Young's greatest albums but, far from being the bonkers turkey of popular perception, it was a courageous, innovative work that merits a significant footnote in the development of electronic music. Even if the album was a failure – at least it was a heroic one.

Not that David Geffen agreed. He wanted something he could sell, and had no compunction about telling Neil as much. And when Neil then went off and made a country record – *Old Ways* – Geffen hit the roof. "That wouldn't sell," he said. No way was Neil releasing a country album. Geffen wanted a *rock 'n' roll* album. Give him a rock 'n' roll album.

A resentful, frustrated, raging Young took Geffen at his word. A European tour playing the *Trans* material proved a further disaster – financially, artistically and mentally – and Young then went hell for leather in the opposite direction, knocking out *Everybody's Rockin'* – an almost cartoon-esque 1950s rockabilly pastiche seemingly made for the express purpose of winding up David Geffen.

It worked. David Geffen was *very* wound up.

The cover art alone – a comic image of Young in white suit, black shirt and pink tie, standing in classic rock 'n' roll pose with slicked-back hair against a sickly pink wall under the banner of "Neil & The Shocking Pinks" was itself a thumb in the face of his bombastic, dictatorial master. The album – barely 25 minutes of it – was full of throwaway rockabilly, like "Betty Lou's Got A Band New Pair Of Shoes" (a minor Bobby Freeman hit from 1958), Jimmy Reed's 1961 blues howler "Bright Lights, Big City", and a 1953 song that became closely associated with Elvis, "Mystery Train", alongside a smattering of Young originals which sounded like deliberate clichés of the genre.

Geffen *did* put this one out. And it bombed. Appallingly. Sales of the previous three albums had been relatively poor, but *Everybody's Rockin'* didn't even make it to the Top 40 in the US or the UK. And as soon as he saw the dreadful sales figures, Geffen reacted in the way he best knew how. He talked to his lawyers.

Neil suddenly found himself on the receiving end of a lawsuit. Geffen was claiming $3.3m damages over the content of both the *Trans* and *Everybody's Rockin'* albums, which he claimed weren't commercial enough or characteristic of Neil's previous work. In essence, he was accusing Young of fraud; of selling him a dummy.

Geffen had signed Young as the flagship artist of his new label at a huge price in the belief that he would repay him with a record that would not only be a slice of pure genius but be recognized as such by the great public, and in turn make the label a fortune. Two unequivocal flops later, and Geffen decided he'd been stitched up and that somebody had to pay. That somebody, clearly, was the misfiring genius himself, Neil Young.

That misfiring genius wouldn't be bullied and stood up to be counted. Neil filed an even bigger countersuit against Geffen, accusing him of breach of contract by not allowing the complete artistic freedom he'd promised at the outset. Two giants in their own way – the hardheaded businessman and the bullheaded artist – stood toe to toe and slugged it out. And it all got very ugly.

Artists constantly fall out with their record companies, at which point the writs start to fly, but an artist of the stature of Neil Young being sued by the record label he was still signed to – essentially for not selling enough records – was something else. The idea of a powerful businessman like Geffen using the law to attack Young – the tortured artist – appealed to a popular perception about evil record company bosses routinely exploiting the sensitive musician chasing the elusive muse. Public support swung behind Neil, who did nothing to counter the popular illusion of him as an innocent victim.

There's only one winner in this situation – the lawyers – and after huge arguments, immense mental stress, and endless soul-searching on both sides, Geffen backtracked, issuing an apology to Neil not only for serving the suit, but for interfering with his artistic freedom. He later tried to justify the lawsuit, claiming it was a case of tough love; his own crafty psychological ploy to shock Young into making ever better music, but it wasn't an argument that held much sway with anyone, least of all Young, whose own "penalty" was being forced to fulfil the rest of his five-album contract to Geffen.

Whatever else he was, Young was now also a champion of free speech and a romantic hero to all who supported the notion of art above commerce – always a key element of his creed.

In a warped way, the surrounding publicity had given Neil's image a boost. The downside was that the whole sorry episode had taken a lot out of Neil – physically, mentally and financially – and there were times during those 18 months when some thought he was considering giving up music completely. But ultimately, it empowered Neil and, in terms

Neil's shirts stayed roughly consistent throughout his career, but his taste in hats changed like the wind.

The early 1980s ushered in Young's "vocoder years" along with his most baffling album, *Trans*.

of creating whatever type of music he wanted, it made him invincible. It was official: nobody told Neil Young what he could or couldn't do.

The immediate consequence was the release of *Old Ways*, the country album previously shelved by Geffen because it wasn't considered commercial enough. "The longer you sue me for playing country music the longer I'm going to play country music," said Young provocatively. "Either you back off or I'm going to play country music forever."

So he put together a new band, the International Harvesters, awash with fiddles, banjos and pedal steel, and went off on the road playing country music as, after a two year hiatus since *Everybody's Rockin'*, *Old Ways* hit the stores. The perfect symmetry to complete Young's emergence as giant-killing hero would be for *Old Ways* to be a runaway success, vindicating his stubborn resistance to corporate pressure and confirming the image of Geffen as a clueless suit.

Sadly this didn't happen. Despite the presence on the album of country greats like Waylon Jennings and Willie Nelson, the new hillbilly Neil Young was received with even less rapture than the rockabilly Neil of *Everybody's Rockin'* and the techno Neil of *Trans*.

Yet Neil wanted to prove a point, and was more committed to *Old Ways* than almost anything he'd ever done before, throwing himself into the live performances and even uncharacteristically undertaking a spate of promotional interviews in which he enthusiastically reasserted his belief in all the flag-waving values of family, loyalty and morality that middle America holds so dear, and again he spoke supportingly of Ronald Reagan: "So what if he's a trigger happy cowboy? He hasn't pulled the trigger," was one of his more contentious outbursts.

Neil also eagerly championed the merits of country music over rock 'n' roll. "I think in some ways rock 'n' roll has let me down," he told journalist Adam Sweeting. "It really doesn't leave you a way to grow old gracefully and continue to work. If you're gonna rock you better burn out 'cause that's the way they wanna see you."

After years of trying to get him to promote himself via interviews, manager Elliot Roberts was now doing his best to shut Neil up for fear of what he might say and who he might alienate next in his pro-Reagan outbursts, which were comprehensively destroying his whole ethos as an individual leftist artist with a burning social conscience and the moral courage to fight for what he believed in. The arch wind-up merchant, Neil was playacting half the time anyway and having great fun doing it, with no recourse to the long-term ramifications for his career and public persona.

Emotive and newsworthy quotes tend to dog public figures – particularly in the age of the Internet – without reference to the circumstances, the tone, the frame of mind, or the motivation behind them, and there are people even now who believe Young is a rabid redneck Republican, even though he is essentially apolitical, switching his opinions depending on the wind direction. None of this mattered to Young, of course, deliriously riding on the cowboy train that would self-destruct his career, but it mattered to Elliot Roberts. "No more interviews," Roberts told him, "please Neil, *no more interviews*."

Yet Neil's love of pure country music is genuine, as later evinced by his work a quarter of a century later. *Treasure* was a live album taken from Neil's International Harvesters tours of the mid-1980s. "Real country music played by real country musicians," he told *Rolling Stone* in 2011, still sounding as if he bore a grudge against the country music world that had failed to give him credence the first time around. "The people in control who played music on the radio were sure that I shouldn't be doing what I was doing. But it didn't matter to me. I kept on doing it anyway."

Neil's theory about the world at large wanting their rock stars to burn out rather than grow old gracefully is an interesting one, in part born out by the later tragedy in which he became indirectly embroiled – the death of Kurt Cobain. Yet Young himself, of course, has gone on to disprove the theory in his own inimitable fashion. And he didn't take too long disrobing from his country clothes, spending much of the rest of the 1980s cleansing himself

RIGHT: Neil with his three favourite items – fancy guitar, fancy car and fancy hat.

OPPOSITE: Neil young croons like some sort of ghostly apparition, as he possesses London's infamous Wembley Stadium.

of the turmoil and turbulence of the Geffen experience, reclaiming his own territory and viewing the past anew.

Prompted by the desperate drug problems, and a prison sentence, hanging over the head of his old comrade David Crosby, Neil directly addressed the failures of the Woodstock generation while defiantly celebrating his own determination to survive on the poignant "Hippie Dream" from the 1986 album *Landing On Water*: "Just because it's over for you, don't mean it's over for me. It's a victory for the heart, every time the music starts."

Not that *Landing On Water* was any great shakes or did anything to help Neil's faded commercial stock, but Young's mindset did seem markedly more positive after his various travails including his son's situation; financial woes; the stand-off with Geffen; and a court case involving *Human Highway* – a self-financed (to the tune of $3m) foray into the world of movie making (under the pseudonym Bernard Shakey) which rebounded badly on Neil when actress Sally Kirkland sued after her co-star Dennis Hopper accidentally cut one of her tendons with a knife on set.

After everything that had happened, Young was ready to shake hands with, if not completely embrace, his former self. There was a Buffalo Springfield reunion for one thing; a tour with his old mates Crazy Horse; another kiss and make-up with CSNY, resulting in a happy reunion for them at the first Bridge School benefit concert.

Neil's Geffen hell finally came to an end with *Life*, a fairly ordinary and listless album by Neil's standards on which he left Geffen with no doubt about his lingering contempt, with a sleeve pointedly depicting the artist imprisoned behind bars. He also left one final poisonous parting shot in the grooves, a track called "Prisoners of Rock 'n' Roll" – a less-than-veiled reference to the chains Neil felt had been attached to him through most of the decade. The Geffen-directed barbs came thick and fast: "We never listen to the record company man, they try to change us and ruin our band"; "We don't wanna be watered down, taking orders from a record company clown"; "That's why we don't wanna be good, we're prisoners of rock 'n' roll."

Bitter? Surely not.

Life represented Neil's commercial nadir. It was the lowest-selling album of his career, and you fondly imagine he was actually quite pleased about that as he ran back into the arms of the label he knew he should never have left in the first place, Reprise.

Yet he still seemed determined to self-destruct, blowing the perfect opportunity to catapult his career back on track when he appeared at the Philadelphia leg of *Live Aid*, Bob Geldof's extraordinary global concert to alleviate starvation in Africa, which spiralled into the biggest and most significant event in music history. Where acts like Queen, U2 and Status Quo shrewdly seized the day with rip-roaring, grandstanding sets that regenerated their careers at a stroke, Neil Young comprehensively wasted his own opportunity to do exactly the same.

"Hits" – that's what they wanted. This crowd wanted hits. Naturally, Neil failed to give them any. In fact, he failed miserably on two counts: a CSNY reunion swiftly sank without trace in an impenetrable haze of sound problems while his own hick performance with the International Harvesters went down like a lead balloon.

Yet, like a lot of other people, Geldof's vision opened Neil's eyes to the power of music to have a positive influence on a cause close to their hearts. At *Live Aid*, Bob Dylan's own rambling and rather dire performance had included a reference to struggling farmers in America, with a suggestion that something should be done for them too. Still in full country mode, this was something that Neil could relate to. *Farm Aid* became Young's baby – a benefit concert he co-founded that year that is still running today.

Suddenly there was a new purpose to Neil, and his senses were on fire in a way they hadn't been for years. And he became a rock 'n' roller again.

Neil's fallow period wasn't yet over. *This Note's For You*, an R&B influenced album marking Neil's return to Reprise, was notable mostly for a Julien Temple video for the title track. It was an attack on corporate sponsorship of music: "Ain't singing for Pepsi, ain't singing for Coke, makes me look like a joke," which, among other things, parodied Michael Jackson's hair catching fire while filming a TV ad. It was banned by MTV after legal threats from Jacko's people, inciting Neil to call MTV "spineless jerks", voraciously biting one of the hands that feeds yet again. He's rarely been shown on MTV since.

Christening his new band the Bluenotes didn't help, either, rousing Harold Melvin (of Harold Melvin & the Bluenotes) to threaten legal action unless he dropped the name.

Same old Neil, rocking and raging and getting up everyone's nose, angry, irascible, illogical, unpredictable, ornery. But somewhere along the line he started to re-discover his real self and - more importantly to those around him - connected again with the public at large. How? He wrote an anthem.

Right at the end of the decade from hell, Neil was about to turn it all around again with one stonking, fist-pumping, right-on, fully-loaded, hard-rocking message of triumph and hope…

After years of trying to beg, bully and coax a hit out of him, David Geffen must have wept when he heard it.

And Neil Young the miracle man was ready to come back from the abyss.

LEFT: Crazy or just misunderstood? Neil ripped apart the rock 'n' roll rulebook through the 1980s.

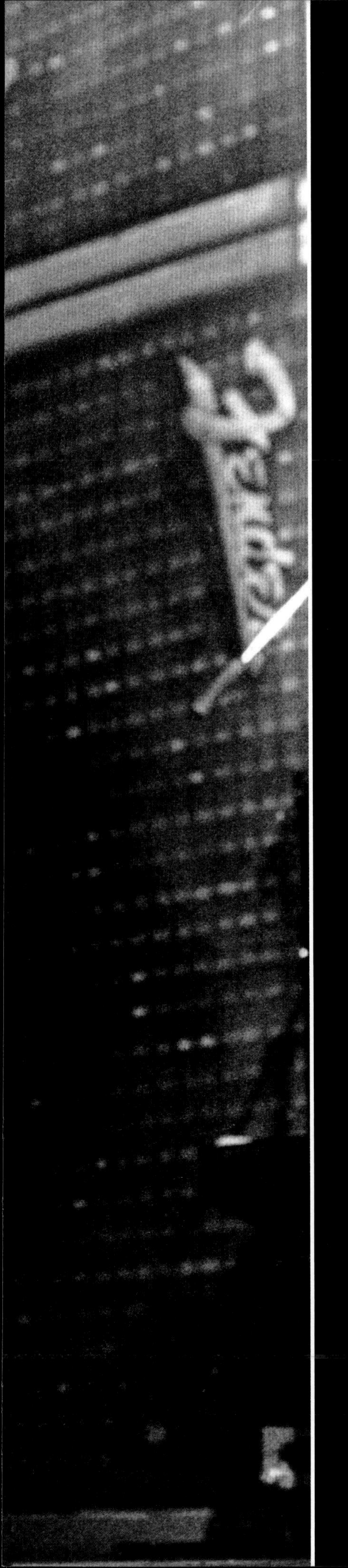

CHAPTER 5

ROCKIN' IN THE FREE WORLD

Ludwig

Brrrrrrrrrrhhhh … buzzzz … zzrrchhkkk … weerrhuummmmmmmmmm … crackle … WHHHHHHHHHAAAAAAAAAAREEEEEEE…

Neil Young plugged himself into the 1990s in a way his contemporaries could only dream of. Most of the stale, old rock dinosaurs had been blown away by punk, and the remaining established superstars were starting to look like tired, waxwork imitations of themselves.

Rock was dead, lying in a pool of its own hairspray – but Young was not about to go gently into the night; this old beast was about to go CGI. Bathing in a headstorm of feedback, his distorted anthems and forlorn visions of the world would light a fire in the soul of a new generation and return stadium rock to its most primal, gut-bleeding best. Hey hey, my, oh, my.

Young was a brooding character then (when wasn't he?). Years of butting heads with Geffen had come to an end, he'd re-signed to Reprise, and his mix of anger, frustration and disdain for the music industry … the world … the system … was fit to burst.

Commercially, he was at his lowest ebb, critically, he was a laughing stock, and his 1988 reunion with Crosby, Stills and Nash had ended uneasily with a cocaine-fuelled Stephen Stills toting guns and ranting madly about his role in the Vietnam War (the fact that he was playing guitar in Buffalo Springfield at the time seemed neither here nor there.)

The world was changing too. The Berlin Wall was about to tumble, recession was about to hit the US, and the Gulf War was brewing. Young was ticking, and a big, volatile release of tension, angst and pent-up creative energy was ready to explode. It was time to turn the amps up to 11 and let it all out.

The first chink of light came with the release of the tribute album *The Bridge* (1989), featuring cover versions of Young's songs by Sonic Youth, Nick Cave, The Pixies, The Flaming Lips, Dinosaur Jr., and a host of new bands. Young had managed to alienate himself from just about everyone in the industry at the time, and was generally regarded as a grumpy, eccentric, old rock relic not to be touched with a barge pole – so a tribute album came as a bit of a shock. He initially dismissed it, assuming it to be a sendup, but soon discovered an unlikely kinship with this new generation.

The screeching guitars, the sense of alienation, and the artistic, anti-corporate ethos of the growing alternative scene appealed to Neil's sensibilities, and chimed musically with the crunching distortion of the limited edition album *Eldorado* which was barely noticed when he released it at the end of 1988.

And so, with the times a-changin', the dread festering, and the chips down, Young produced his finest work in years with the

LEFT: Reunited with Crazy Horse – Neil the rocker is reborn.

classic *Freedom* (1989). Seen as a follow-up, sister album to *Rust Never Sleeps* a decade earlier, the surges of thrashing electricity from Young's howling guitars sat starkly against cinematic Nashville ballads and lost highway chases, as the whole notion of freedom and the American dream was taken to task.

The open road, inner-city degradation, consumer culture, politics, religion and patriotism all raced through Young's thoughts as he dissected the nation's psyche and what he saw as the illusion of freedom. This was a warts 'n' all picture postcard of the US from the Bruce Springsteen school of Americana rock operas, bookended with two versions of Young's glorious retort to "Born in the USA" – "Rockin' in the Free World".

Just as the Boss's barbed anthem had been misunderstood as a chest-beating call to arms, "Rockin' in the Free World" was a desperate warning of growing problems both abroad and in the US, masked with a driving riff, a breakneck guitar solo, and a pumping, lung-busting chorus.

According to Young's biographer Jimmy McDonough, the idea came when Young and Crazy Horse guitarist Frank Sampedro saw pictures of the dead body of Iranian leader Ayatollah Khomeini being carried through the streets of post-revolutionary Iran. As mourners burned US flags, Sampedro reportedly turned to Young and said: "Whatever we do, we shouldn't go near the Middle East. It's probably better we just keep on rocking in the free world."

The sentiment of the song could have been straight out of the 1960s protest movement. The spirit of Young's days as a folkie playing Winnipeg coffee houses was plugged in, and pumped out to a new era. Yet, the opaque political message and the invoked sense of nationalistic pride confused the issue. "The song is a lot of images of the destruction in our streets, the homelessness and drugs and war and all these Muslims hating us, Americans and Europeans. We're like the devil to them," Young told Q magazine in 1989. "I'm just describing both sides like a journalist. There's no answer from me, no guidance. I just write what I think I see and I change my own mind about it every day."

These prophetic warnings about the ill-feeling towards the West would later tragically ring true, but at the time, they became muddled within tales of social degradation and decay. Look closely, and it's a pretty dystopian vision of America's streets, but it soon gets blown away by that big, booming chorus and scorching fret work. This is a spiritual cousin to Jimi Hendrix tearing through the "Star Spangled Banner" while war raged in Vietnam. It's Bob Dylan electrifying folk songs. It's Young delivering his own brand

LEFT: Neil on stage with Willie Nelson, who played with him on the *Old Ways* album in 1985.

of patriotism, wrapping himself in the Stars and Stripes and raging with the contradictions of fear, pride, shame and anger.

Neil's return to form was marked with a blisteringly intense live performance of the song on the TV show *Saturday Night Live* – now regarded as one of his great moments. Hiring a personal trainer to give him an hour-long workout before going onstage, Young's blood was surging as he slashed and thrashed like a man possessed. In the 1960s – the apocryphal legend went that Pete Seeger tried to take an axe to Bob Dylan's amp to stop him going electric. It would have taken a nuclear bomb to stop Young this night.

As the Cold War began to thaw, the song took on huge significance right across Europe as well. Newsreaders delivered their reports about the fall of the Berlin Wall to camera with all due sincerity, while clusters of people leapt all over the concrete divide in the background, and Neil Young came screeching out of tinny little speakers.

David Hasselhoff's somewhat crasser single "Looking For Freedom" was also a big hit, and it was he who pranced around the Brandenburg Gate later that year at a New Year's Eve party dressed in fairy lights and a piano-key scarf claiming to have united Germany. If they had sent for Young with his huge amp stacks, leather jacket, and storms of howling feedback, they wouldn't have needed a wrecking ball to tear that wall down.

The success of *Freedom* propelled Young back into the spotlight. He was now idolized by the new guard, but was also welcomed back with open arms into the conscience of mainstream classic-rock fans. Somehow he'd managed to become both an arty outsider and stadium-filling headliner without ever really seeking to be either.

Striking up a friendship with the self-anointed kingmaker of the new scene Thurston Moore, Neil toured, with Sonic Youth supporting, and was soon recognized as a key inspiration for this new, untamed, DIY, primal sound. By the time Nirvana had exploded into the charts with the ticking-time-bomb-of-youth anthem "Smells Like Teen Spirit", Young had been crowned "Don Grungio – the Godfather of Grunge".

It's a title Neil accepted with his usual mix of good grace and self-conscious embarrassment, but his love and respect for the bands of that time shone through. One look at him on stage then – and still *now* – and you can see in an instant how much he was affected by the era. The slick pop star sheen of the 1980s had never really sat right, but now Neil could just unleash a more primitive sound.

The straggly hair coursing with static, the torn jeans, the plaid shirts, and the unholy barrage pouring out of the speakers was perfectly in sync with the new wave of stars. Hunched over his axe,

RIGHT: Three Just Men explore Americana: Neil Young, Kris Kristofferson and Willie Nelson.

FREE
PELTIER

chopping and pounding away to his heart's content, Young was given a new lease of life, and he was quick to share it with his old mates Crazy Horse.

Despite vowing to never play with the band again after a falling out on their *Rusted Out Garage* tour in 1987, Neil reunited with them three years later for the *Ragged Glory* album. Young's sprawling new sound had more of a groove and strut than before, and the band's deep-rooted understanding from years of playing together added a looser, more instinctive feel to the proceedings.

It was if the band were back in their garages as teenagers playing for the genuine love of it, free from record-company pressures, egos or addictions. Recorded at Young's ranch in Northern California, there was a jammed-out sound and revved-up sense of fun as the old mates ran through reworkings of "Country Home" and "White Line" – both songs that originally appeared in the 1970s – and a clattering, bar-room cover of the R&B standard "Farmer John".

Living up to its name, *Ragged Glory* feeds off of scores of scruffy licks, blistering solos, and indulgent 10-minute beasts like "Love To Burn" and "Love and Only Love". Apart from raising environmental concerns on "Mother Earth (Natural Anthem)", the social commentary was largely dropped, as Young and the band unshackled themselves to bask in skuzzy, three-chord rock 'n' roll tracks like "Fuckin' Up" and "Mansion On The Hill". The grunge bands had drawn inspiration from the raw power and unprogrammed excitement of Young's classic 1979 album *Rust Never Sleeps*, and here he was – a generation later – giving it back to them with added ferocity. There was still life in the grizzled, old hippy yet, and he wasn't about to let the young whippersnappers have all the fun.

Neil toured the album successfully and released the live album *Weld*, accompanied by an avant-garde sound collage of screeching feedback and crashing noise called *Arc*. But when things couldn't get any louder, it was time for another contradictory handbrake turn.

All that rockin' in the free world in front of 2,000-watt banks of speakers had left Young with tinnitus – a condition that causes a ringing in the ears and a painful reaction to loud noise – not ideal considering the prolific run of form he'd hit with his apocalyptic new sound. "The physical thing with feedback, y'know, it takes its toll on you when you play really loud," he told the NME in 1992. "I kept thinking, aww, pretty soon I'm going to have to think of something else."

It was time to unplug.

Neil looked back to his days as a folkie, and at his country roots, for some soothing lullabies, and finally made peace with his greatest success (and the album that haunted him most) – *Harvest*. After 20 years of record executives imploring him to make a follow-up, Neil finally felt at ease enough with himself and the world around him to record a sequel. He gathered up Linda Ronstadt, James Taylor, Jack Nitzsche and other contributors to the 1972 best-seller, dug out the melancholic voice and warm, campfire acoustics, and made *Harvest Moon*.

Legendary session player Spooner Oldham also contributed heavily on piano and organ as Young, in dreamy, nostalgic mood, gently reminisced, like he was raising a glass to old friends. *Harvest Moon*, he said, was about making things last, and carrying the past with you. Or, as he told Allan Jones, "it's about the feeling that you don't have to be young to be young…"

Amid the lush, pipe-and-slippers cosiness of *Harvest Moon* there's a bittersweet sense of yearning – it's like a full moon rising, as Young sits on his verandah, surveying his ranch and watching the sun go down, every inch the happy homesteader. Lap steel guitar shimmers atmospherically as Neil ushers us deep into Americana roots – dusty roads, Harley Davidsons, and vivid childhood memories. The banjo is out for "Old King", a tribute to Neil's pet dog (named Elvis, naturally), and he romantically invokes the past on "You and Me" before ending with "Natural Beauty" – a 10-minute *After the Gold Rush* ode to old flames and apple pie America.

Culturally, *Harvest Moon* was at complete odds with the musical climate of the time; with MTV; with Neil's new pals on the grunge scene, and that may have been precisely the reason Neil decided the time was at last right to revisit the setting that made him a superstar, with all the baggage that came with it. "I made *Harvest Moon* because I didn't want to hear any loud sounds," was his pragmatic explanation in an interview with *Mojo* magazine.

It may have been completely out of sync with the times, but Young got behind *Harvest Moon* in a way he'd done with few previous albums, exposing himself to numerous interviews and TV appearances to support his label's big promotional push. And it did the trick. *Harvest Moon* was a hit, leading Neil to self-deprecatingly refer to it as his "Perry Como phase", and in the process inspiring a whole new generation touched by the project's simple beauty, rustic charm, and dusty melancholia. Conor Oberst, Elliot Smith, Mumford and Sons, Ryan Adams, and a growing band of singer-songwriters, all drank deeply from the well of *Harvest Moon*, and flourished as a result.

It may not have quite recreated the mammoth sales of its spiritual predecessor (and glory knows, Neil certainly wouldn't have wanted *that*) but it put him back into the bestsellers, and its influence spread far and wide. TV on the Radio's Tunde Adebimpe covered the track

RIGHT: Neil adopts his undertaker look.

"Unknown Legend" for the film *Rachel Getting Married* in 2008, and the album's tentacles spread into some unlikely areas with an influence felt more and more as the years passed. Suddenly, Neil found himself getting invited onstage with any number of younger artists he'd barely heard of. He was being asked to contribute to soundtracks of hot new movies, or to record with everyone from Pearl Jam to Booker T & The MGs. Mostly, Neil said no. He had no intention of getting back on that old merry-go-round.

Young likes to compare his works to paintings hanging in a gallery, knowing their value will really be judged years down the line, and that rings especially true of *Harvest Moon*. Initially regarded as a bizarre, retro move back to his folkie roots, it now ranks not only among the upper echelons of his greatest commercial successes, but as yet another landmark along the winding road of Young's career.

"My biggest enemy is my own history," he said once, but the agreeable experience of *Harvest Moon* helped him come to terms with it, and he continued to confront his own history, maintaining the acoustic tenderness with a highly acclaimed session for MTV's *Unplugged* series in 1993. Delving into his back catalogue, Neil performed a career-spanning set that included Buffalo Springfield's "Mr Soul", and the classics "Like A Hurricane" and "The Needle and the Damage Done", then a wistful version of *Harvest Moon*, and, to finish off, a road-weary rendition of another *Harvest Moon* track, "From Hank to Hendrix", his highly personalized account of his own journey.

The world apparently couldn't get enough of Neil Young all of a sudden and, despite reports of more tension within Team Young (plus unhappiness with the way the album was recorded), *Harvest Moon Unplugged* was not only acclaimed by critics and fans, it was another best-seller, reaching the dizzy heights of No. 4 in the UK Top 40 Album Charts.

Neil's performance and the enthusiastic reaction it inspired helped to establish the *Unplugged* format as a ratings winner, paving the way for a flood of bands to pick up acoustic guitars and follow Neil's lead. Among them was a band already in thrall to him, Nirvana. It proved to be one of the most brilliant and memorable of all the *Unplugged* performances, and for Nirvana, one of their last…

On Friday, April 8, 1994, Kurt Cobain was found dead from a self-inflicted shotgun wound to the head. The last line of his suicide note contained the now infamous line from Young's 1979 single "Hey Hey, My My (Into the Black)" – "It's better burn out than to fade away."

Troubled by heroin addiction and personal problems, Cobain stood as a creative outsider who'd always struggled with the pressures of his fame, just as Young had done. A generation mourned one of its most iconic voices in a huge outpouring of grief – rock 'n' roll had lost another brilliant, troubled soul to a mixture of drugs and depression.

The leading figure in the grunge movement choosing a Neil Young lyric to express the reason for his suicide had a profound effect on Neil.

Young and Cobain had never met, but their mutual admiration was huge. A love of heavy distorted guitars, a sense of artistic integrity, and a shy, unassuming mistrust of fame and celebrity made the pair lost artistic soulmates. They even shared the same penchant for torn jeans and scruffy, oversized checked shirts.

"He really, really inspired me. He was so great. Wonderful…" Young said of Cobain, in an interview with Nick Kent for *Mojo* in 1995. "He was one of the best, but more than that, Kurt was one of the absolute greats of all time for me."

On the days leading up to Kurt's death, Young had tried to phone Cobain several times to arrange a meeting. He'd just returned from a tour with Booker T and the MGs and was halfway through recording a new album with Crazy Horse, but had been listening a lot to the new, alternative bands. With his hearing problems much improved, Neil was ready to rock again, and fresh material like "Piece of Crap" and "Blue Eden" pointed at his return to a more raucous, jammed-out sound.

But Cobain's death changed the whole mood of the album. "I like to think I could have done something," Young told *The Guardian*'s Burhan Wazir in 2002. "I was just trying to reach him. Trying to connect with him. It's just too bad I didn't get a shot. I had an impulse to connect. Only when my song was used in that suicide note was the connection made. Then, I felt it was really unfortunate that I didn't get through to him. I might have been able to make things a little lighter for him, that's all. Just lighten it up a little bit."

Neil was plagued by parallels between the deaths of Kurt Cobain and Neil's old Crazy Horse cohort Danny Whitten. They were physically similar for one thing. Both had straggly, dirty blond hair and blue eyes; both had come from divorced families; both were massively talented; both had become addicted to heroin; lost their way; and plunged into a chronic depression.

When Whitten died in 1972, Young and Crazy Horse paid tribute with the tequila-fuelled, grief-stricken album *Tonight's The Night*. This time, the sessions the band were working on turned into the 1994 album *Sleeps With Angels* – a fitting personal tribute led by the atmospheric, doomed grind of the eponymous track and the wounded, heartbroken plea of "Change Your Mind".

Guilt, sadness and confusion weighed heavily on Young's shoulders, and the painful guilt and sense of responsibility he'd always felt over Whitten's death quickly resurfaced. His memories of firing Whitten – sending him on his way with $50 and a plane ticket home – reverberated once more, the shock and agony doubled by the discovery that Cobain's suicide note quoted Neil's lyric.

Kurt had misinterpreted Neil Young's meaning of those words, for Neil had written "Hey Hey, My My (Into the Black)" as a tribute to the energy of punk, and as a statement of intent that "rock 'n' roll will never die". And whenever Neil performed the song in future, he put all of his emphasis on the line "once you're gone, you can't come back…"

Sleeps With Angels turned out to be a cathartic experience for Young, capturing the dark melancholia of the era, once more tapping into the mood of the day. As a result, the album was another big success, reaching No. 9 on the US charts, while furthering Neil's connection with the grunge scene, and paving the way for him to work with Pearl Jam on his next album *Mirror Ball* in 1995.

Young had been friends with Pearl Jam's Eddie Vedder for a few years, performing a storming version of "Keep On Rockin' in the Free World" with him at the 1993 MTV Music Video Awards. Despite Cobain's derision of Pearl Jam, and his accusation that they were "pioneering a corporate, alternative cock-rock fusion," Young became a firm fan. And when Neil was inducted into the Rock and Roll Hall of Fame in January, 1995, it was Vedder who gave a heartfelt inauguration speech for his hero.

LEFT: Jim Jarmusch – director of *Dead Man* starring Johnny Depp – had Neil Young compose and perform its score, before filming Neil's tour documentary *Year of the Horse*.

ABOVE: The devil in Neil Young and (RIGHT) in a more familiar pose.

PERIPHERALS
WITH
Continental

"He has taught us a lot as a band about dignity and commitment and playing in the moment," Vedder told the audience at the ceremony, later adding: "I don't know if there's an artist that has been inducted into the Rock and Roll Hall of Fame to commemorate a career that is still as vital as he is today."

Failing to live up to Vedder's prediction that his acceptance speech would trash the music industry suits, Young cast his cynicism aside for one night and, looking remarkably smart, was surprisingly emotional as he blinked into the face of a standing ovation, thanking everyone from his mum to Ahmet Ertegun, Elliot Roberts, his wife Pegi, and Crazy Horse, even choking up as he said "I'd like to thank Kurt Cobain for giving me inspiration to renew my commitments."

Neil also united with fellow inductees Led Zeppelin on stage with him for a roaring rendition of "When The Levee Breaks" that saw a mighty meeting of two guitar gods, as Young and Jimmy Page launched into a high-octane fretwork duel. A few days later, Neil performed with Pearl Jam at an abortion-rights benefit rally in Washington, before they entered the Bad Animals Studio in Seattle together. The collaboration was a frantic, raw collision of driving guitars and feedback, chronicling a theme which Young described as a drift in idealism from the free love days of the 1960s to the cynicism rife among the '90s Generation X.

It was a triumphant alliance. The grizzled, outcast gunslinger and his roaring disciples took their cues from the Cinema Verité form of film-making to recreate the free-form jam session that had proved so successful on 1975's classic *Tonight's The Night*. Pearl Jam were a ferociously joyous backing band filling the boots of Crazy Horse as they thrashed out a thundering groove to make an album largely written and recorded in just four days.

The gloom and despondency that had consumed Young the previous year was completely blown away in those four days recording *Mirror Ball*. Young's fresh, buoyant mood was captured well by the lead single "Downtown", that name-dropped Led Zeppelin, Jimi Hendrix and Jimmy Page in a foot-stomping Saturday night boogie. With the rock world still mourning Kurt Cobain, it seemed as if Neil Young – growing into the role of rock's senior citizen – had decided to inject a note of optimism, hope and fun back into music. Neil Young on a crusade for positivity and optimism ... now that was a first.

Across the pond in the UK, the post-grunge party had already started, with a gang of Mancunians calling themselves Oasis setting the music world alight with their anthem "Live Forever" that provided a swaggering response to Cobain's suicide. Britpop was starting to restore a sense of confidence, attitude and cool to the national zeitgeist and America, too, seemed more economically and politically content under President Clinton after some sticky years.

Nirvana drummer Dave Grohl was gearing up to launch his new band Foo Fighters and, as ever, Young was at the centre of things in Seattle – the home of grunge – stating that it was time to move on.

Pearl Jam have spoken about the experience of working with Neil Young. Neil may have got a great album out of the collaboration, but he rejuvenated Pearl Jam too, as together they worked the driving engine room that produced tracks like "Big Green Country", "Throw Your Hatred Down" and "Scenery".

Eddie Vedder's contribution was restricted by a troublesome stalker, but he did cowrite and duet on the centrepiece "Peace and Love" and sang lead on outtakes "I Got Id" and "Long Road" that made it onto the follow-up *Merkin Ball* EP.

The album may have tackled darker issues, such as abortion on the tracks "Song X" and "Act of Love", but it's remembered as a forceful, hard-rocking celebration of the Godfather of Grunge and his young disciples. Young himself described it best in an interview with Mark Cooper for Q Magazine in 1995 when he said: "Recording *Mirror Ball* was like audio verité, just a snapshot of what's happening. Sometimes I didn't know who was playing. I was just conscious of this big smouldering mass of sound."

The flames of that smouldering mass were fanned a few months later when Pearl Jam were playing the biggest gig of their career in front of 50,000 people at Golden Gate Park, San Francisco. Young was waiting in the wings, ready to join them for an encore when, after 30 minutes, Vedder limped offstage complaining of severe stomach flu. Step forward Don Grungio, with faithful axe Old Black at the ready, to take his place in what became a blistering 90-minute set of *Mirror Ball* tracks and classic Young hits. The altered lineup was subsequently dubbed "Crazier Horse".

Pearl Jam were forced to cancel further shows, but the moment of the night came as the sweat-drenched, 49-year-old, grizzled hippy delivered the killer line from "I'm The Ocean" – "People my age, they don't do the things I do," which made even the pent-up, teenage Pearl Jam fans (who were previously demanding their money back) raise a smile.

LEFT: Neil Young and his beloved gas-guzzling 1959 Lincoln Continental that he converted into an eco-friendly automobile running on clean fuel.

FOLLOWING PAGE TOP LEFT: Neil in full flight with his trustiest companion, "Old Black", his Les Paul guitar.

FOLLOWING PAGE BELOW LEFT: Neil's anticipation for his future projects remained palpable.

FOLLOWING PAGE RIGHT: Neil celebrates his return to Reprise with the *Freedom* album, his biggest success for years.

Neil Young had proved himself not only as one of rock's ultimate survivors – he was one of its supreme leaders and innovators – an inspirational guiding star to successive new generations. The man, clearly, was invincible.

Neil could do whatever he liked and still be adored, and by the middle of the 1990s he was recording an instrumental soundtrack for director Jim Jarmusch's western *Dead Man*. After this, Neil teamed up with Crazy Horse for another jammed-out, journey into beefy, heart-on-sleeve rock 'n' roll.

Broken Arrow – their seventh album together – led to the classic Jarmusch-directed concert film and live album *Year of the Horse*, before another reunion with Crosby, Stills and Nash produced *Looking Forward* (1999) and a huge tour of the US and Canada which grossed $42 million.

The defining image of the era, though, is of a middle-aged man with crazy hair hunched over his guitar, feedback crackling out of huge speaker stacks. Neil Percival Young – grizzled guitar god – rockin' in the free world in all his ragged glory...

ABOVE: Whenever this man touched an axe, magical things started to happen, seen here in Finsbury Park, London, 1993.

RIGHT: Nuclear power – Neil Young was a powerful star.

CHAPTER 6

TWISTED ROAD

"Let's impeach the President for lying, and misleading our country into war, abusing all the power, and shipping all the money from the door."

"This, *this* music ... is already causing a stir," said CNN reporter Siblia Vargas, using all of her journalistic nous in 2006. "You've got one song that's called 'Let's Impeach the President'. Tell us Neil ... what is the song about?"

From the '60s folkie, to the Reagan-sympathizing patriot, to the raging anti-war protester, the politics of Neil Young have always been a maze of head-scratching contradictions. "Think of me as one you'd never figured out," he sang on the track "Powderfinger", and he wasn't kidding. Neil's views seem to have darted and morphed as often as his musical styles did, but in a decade shaped by the 9/11 atrocities, Young would find an incendiary political voice.

While it was Stephen Stills who penned Buffalo Springfield's ode to the civil rights era – "For What It's Worth" – Young was regarded as something of a lonesome, apolitical figure who may have greatly admired the protest material of Bob Dylan, Phil Ochs and Joan Baez, but didn't allow it to seep into his own work.

In his song "Chicago", Graham Nash even implored Young to join him on marches, but to no avail.

Things didn't change until the 1970 Kent State University killings of protesting students by the National Guard, leading Young to write "Ohio" – his anthem for the counterculture movement – which not only reached No. 14 in the US charts, but marked the man's transformation into a fearless and passionate songwriter.

Particularly striking was the song's direct fingerpointing at the President – "Tin Soldiers and Nixon coming, we're finally on our own, this summer I hear the drumming, four dead in Ohio." To name and shame the President in such a way was unheard of at the time, and showed either genuine courage or a complete disregard for any possible backlash. It soon became clear though that this was no bid to take Dylan's voice-of-a-generation crown; more an outpouring of anger and disgust at the general situation.

Young believed that matters of politics should not interfere with artistic freedom and independence, but as the years passed, we started to hear more of the man's colourful opinions.

Neil spoke openly of his support for many of President Ronald Reagan's initiatives; Neil had a doomed view of American foreign policy; Neil also even admired Nixon on the 1977 track "Campaigner". At heart, Neil's songwriting indicated that he remained a simple, down-to-earth country boy – an adopted US patriot.

Neil's thoughts were sacrilege to the ageing generation of left-leaning activists sickened by the words of someone who was starting to sound like a chest-beating right-wing Republican. Yet in truth, Neil always seemed more at home in the back of a pickup truck with a dog on his lap than he did in the back of Ken Kesey's psychedelic bus, and by the 2000s, he had nurtured a large fan base on both sides of the political divide.

Days after the terrorist attacks brought down the Twin Towers in New York in 2001, Young played an emotional rendition of John Lennon's classic "Imagine" at the *America: A Tribute To Heroes* fundraiser in front of a television audience of 89 million. The plaintive, idealistic hymn was widely recognized as one of the highlights of the night, but the issues facing America and the world were more complex than Lennon could ever have dreamed. Young's response was typically unpredictable...

Teaming up with R&B legends Booker T & the MGs, Young took yet another journey into different musical styles, dabbling with soul, funk, and all things Stax Records, on the album *Are You Passionate?* in 2002. Among a mixed bag of strutting, jammed-out funky rock, it was lead track "Let's Roll" that really stood out.

Telling the story of United Airlines Flight 93 (which was hijacked as part of the 9/11 attacks, but crash landed on its way to Washington) the song pays tribute to the heroism of the passengers who tried to stop the terrorists. Making phone calls from the back of the plane, the passengers heard news of the attacks on the World Trade Center and realized what was happening. They organized themselves, even taking a vote on what to do, and made an attempt to regain control of the plane, ultimately forcing it to crash in a field in Pennsylvania. The final words heard over the phone were the rallying call – "Let's roll."

In the years following the attacks, a collective sense of fear, combined with growing calls for action, and a lust for revenge, produced a tightening of homeland security and the controversial Patriot Act. Fast-tracked into law by President Bush six weeks after 9/11, the legislation introduced a wide range of measures that gave security forces more surveillance powers. It redefined the definition of terrorism to include domestic acts of civil disobedience and rebellion, and it clamped down on immigration.

For liberal thinkers raised on the civil rights traditions, it was a stripping of their freedoms, and a caving in to the fear generated by Al-Qaeda. Young, however, disagreed, and supported the president. "To protect our freedoms it seems as though we're going to have to relinquish some of our freedoms for a short period of time," Young told the campaign group *People for the American Way*, while receiving

LEFT: After 9/11 Neil became an incendiary political voice.

the Spirit of Liberty Award in 2001. These were confusing times, and there were signs they were getting worse.

During the recording sessions of the *Prairie Wind* album in March 2005, Young started suffering from blurred vision and was diagnosed with a brain aneurysm. He recovered quickly and was back onstage for the *Live 8* concert in Ontario, closing the show with a mass singalong of "Rockin' in the Free World" and "O Canada". But the serious nature of the aneurysm put Young in reflective mood, and the Nashville folk rock of *Prairie Wind* took on a similar feel to *Harvest*, wistfully reminiscing and mournfully taking stock of the world, on tracks like "When God Made Me" and "Falling Off the Face of the Earth".

However, dreamy sentimentality soon gave way to frustration, as the war on terror started to look increasingly futile and self-destructive. Moved to tears by newspaper photographs showing a wounded soldier, Young decided it was time for action. Empowered by the confrontation with his own mortality caused by the aneurysm, the gloves came off and Young's rage produced his most furious work since "Ohio".

"I was waiting for someone to come along, some young singer, 18-to-22-years-old, to write these songs and stand up," he told the *Los Angeles Times*. "I waited a long time. Then I decided that maybe the generation that has to do this is still the sixties generation. We're still here."

And do it he did, with a passion and intensity almost shocking for a man approaching 60.

Recorded at Capitol Studios in LA – the birthplace of many Frank Sinatra hits – lead track "Let's Impeach The President" strummed along to the catchiest of tunes before a choir of 100 Musicians Union members united to give it to George W. Bush with both barrels. Laying down a succession of the President's worst offences, the song tackles the untruths told in taking America to war with Iraq; the Patriot Act (that Neil once publicly agreed with); and Bush's disastrous handling of the New Orleans floods.

At a press conference in Berlin two years later, one plucky journalist asked Neil, "What's wrong with Bush?"

"Let's talk about what's *right* with George Bush, because that's a much shorter answer," responded Neil. "I think he's a very good physical specimen. A good example to men his age of how to stay in physical condition." *Ouch*. Neil always had a special way of cutting people down.

Written and recorded in nine days, and released just a month later, the album *Living With War* continued to attack what Young called "metal folk protest music". Drawing an urgent, reactionary

---

RIGHT: Neil Young cuts an imposing figure at a 2008 performance in Vienna, glowing with power and assurance.

line in the sand, "After The Garden" kicked things off with snarling guitars and an apocalyptic view of a post-war world, before "The Restless Consumer" raged about oil, consumerism, a "Madison Avenue War", and a growing conditioning and indifference to the horrors of war.

Far from a calculated and considered argument, the album turned into an instinctive, impassioned rant and an outpouring of anger directed at not only the President but also the futility of the whole situation. It ended with a rendition of "America The Beautiful", expressing Neil's love of the country, and his insistence that opposition to the war didn't make you opposed to the troops or the nation.

That's not how Fox News saw it though.

The right-wing press were soon calling for Young's head, questioning his patriotism, claiming he was jumping on a bandwagon of anti-war sentiment for his own financial gain. They constantly questioned what right a Canadian had to criticize America in the first place. In truth, though, the outrage was low-key compared to the hysteria that the Dixie Chicks caused in 2003 when Natalie Maines declared onstage in England – "We're ashamed that the President of the United States is from Texas."

They were banned from radio stations, death threats piled in, their shows were picketed, sponsors withdrew their support, and fans brought in bulldozers to destroy their CDs. These were sensitive times in which to get political.

In the intervening years, the anti-war voice had risen considerably and, by 2006, Bush's approval rating was at 40%. Three years later it had dropped to 18% – a record low for any president. Yet the backlash on Neil was vicious, and it got worse when he took the *Living With War* album out on tour.

Reuniting with Crosby, Stills and Nash, the *Freedom of Speech* 2006 tour sucked old fans in with the band's classic hits before unleashing the new *Living With War* tracks to a decidedly mixed reaction. Chronicled on the tour DVD, the rockumentary *CSNY/ Déjà Vu* – directed by Young under his pseudonym Bernard Shakey – was a wilfully provocative showpiece that was met with both approval and derision.

The discordant crowds mirrored society's split on the issue of war. Some raised peace signs and sang along to the catchy melodies, while others jeered and walked out spitting feathers: "This whole concert was great until that sonofabitch got that song

ABOVE LEFT: You can't get more high profile than headlining Glastonbury on The Pyramid Stage – all in a night's work for Neil Young.

ABOVE: Dave Matthews and Neil Young performing at the 2010 Hope For Haiti Now concert in Los Angeles.

ABOVE, RIGHT: Growing old disgracefully ... Young entered the new millennium sounding – and looking – more impassioned than ever.

just now on there," cried one happy punter from Atlanta in the film. "I'd like to knock his teeth out."

Young, meanwhile, flourished in the controversy. Convinced that he was on the right path and was backed to the hilt by his old comrades, he didn't give a flying rhubarb what some of Bush's most ardent fans thought or what their disgust might do to his career. At the time there were few dissenting voices within the mainstream music industry, perhaps because of the whole Dixie Chicks palaver. Green Day had hit big with their sneering punk rock concept album *American Idiot* two years earlier, but it's a damning indictment of today's rockers that it took a gang of grizzled, 60-year-old hippies to really shake the hornets' nest. The question, though, that might be asked is where *had* Neil Young the political activist been all his life?

Though never a fully fledged, signed-up, peacenik child of the civil rights movement, Young's social conscience has perhaps been best stirred by Bob Dylan. Not by "Masters Of War" or "Blowing In The Wind" or "Pawn In The Game" or "The Lonesome Death of Hattie Carroll" or any of the other blistering protest songs that had helped make his name in the '60s, but by Dylan's rambling remarks at *Live Aid* in Philadelphia in 1985.

"I hope that some of the money ... maybe they can just take a little bit of it, maybe ... one or two million, maybe ... and use it, say, to pay the mortgages on some of the farms and, the farmers here, owe to the banks..." Dylan had mumbled, to the dismay of concert organizer Bob Geldof, but it did spark something within Young, Willie Nelson and John Mellencamp. *Farm Aid* was the result.

It was a cause that suited Young to a tee. Despite a life spent on the road – living the rock-star dream, touring the great cities of the world, and playing to packed stadiums – Young was always the deep-rooted sort at heart. His upbringing in rural Ontario held fond memories for him, and he generally turned his nose up at glamour girls and other vices in favour of the creature comforts of his 1500-acre ranch in California that he'd called home since 1970. With his ragged jeans, checked shirts and crooked hats, he was immediately at ease with the farmers that *Farm Aid* sought to help. Rallying against big, corporate businesses always came naturally to him anyway.

The first *Farm Aid* show in 1985 used Live Aid as its template, with a stellar lineup of artists including Dylan, Joni Mitchell, Tom Petty, Johnny Cash, Lou Reed, Roy Orbison and Kris Kristofferson – in addition to Nelson, Mellencamp and Young himself – playing to an audience of 80,000 at the University of Illinois Memorial Stadium in Champaign.

It raised over $9 million and went on to play a major role in encouraging the introduction of the Agricultural Credit Act, which helped offer financial assistance at a time when the farming industry was riddled with debt. In more recent times the fund has helped victims of Hurricane Katrina and the 2011 tornadoes, and offered legal and psychological support to those in need.

The energy and determination Young put into *Farm Aid* was revelatory, while the 20th anniversary *Farm Aid* show in 2005 marked him out as something of a visionary too. At the show, a young, little-known Illinois senator spoke admiringly and articulately of the work of the foundation before introducing the next act: folk rockers Wilco. That senator was one Barack Obama.

Young was so impressed that he mentioned Obama in his 2006 song "Looking For A Leader", and years before the senator was ever considered a potential presidential candidate, Neil was singing "Someone walks among us, and I hope he hears the call. Maybe it's a woman, or a black man after all? Maybe it's Obama, but he says he's too young. Maybe it's Colin Powell, to right what he's done wrong."

The philosophy and spirit of *Farm Aid* links to the other big social and political issue close to Young's heart – the environment. Neil's connection with the soil runs deep, and over the years he has become more active on the issue, as the damaging effects of pollution have become more apparent. "When you see a horror movie and you see the birds leave it means something bad is coming," Young warned in an interview with *The Independent* in 2005. "In nature when the birds are depleted and they leave a whole area that means something very big. It's the kind of sign that's lost on politicians."

Young first started to tackle environmental issues on his 2003 concept album *Greendale*. Telling the story of a fictional Californian seaside town, the album became a rock opera featuring a cast of characters whose storylines intertwine in an attempt to tell a wider tale about the modern world and society's ills. It was a typically ambitious and eccentric move for Young to take, but one which was generally regarded as falling on the wrong side of the fine line between genius and Spinal Tap.

Nevertheless, *Greendale* became an all-singing, all-dancing musical stage show, featuring Young and Crazy Horse playing live while a cast of actors enacted the story. Just to make the tour even more kooky, Young decided that the project should be ozone friendly, and he insisted that all trucks and buses be run on bio-diesel fuel. Understandably, the shows were gradually scaled down to an intimate acoustic tour featuring only Young and his wife Pegi.

LEFT: In spite of everything, Neil always remained loyal to his love of hats.

Though hardly an unrivalled success, the experience cemented Neil's eco beliefs, and gave him the determination to pursue his interest in alternative fuels. The brain aneurysm he suffered in 2005 also affected him spiritually, and it stirred his conviction in the matter.

"It gave me more faith. I have faith. I don't know what it is. There's stories that have gone through the ages, and I respect all of them but I don't know where I fit in," he told CNN's Charlie Rose. "I love nature. My church is the forest. I don't have a robe, I don't have a book but I have faith."

Clearly, though, Young was far from your typical tree hugger. An all-American love of power, electricity, and big, grunting, oil-chugging engines stood in stark contrast to the man's conscience. Neil decided to do something about it. His belief in bio-fuel resulted in him driving around town in a huge military-issue H1 Hummer – a behemoth of a vehicle that usually guzzles gas like it's going out of fashion. But Young's monster vehicle was converted to run on vegetable oil, and he took great pleasure in observing disapproving looks change as he rolled down the street. "They think you're the enemy. Then it goes by and they see 'Bio-Diesel', 'Farm-Fuel' and 'Go Earth' written down the side, and they see it's probably cleaner than the car they're driving..."

Putting people's noses out of joint is all in a day's work for the great man, but his passion took him on an even more ambitious mission when he started working on the Lincvolt project in 2007. Recruiting a team of skilled, like-minded engineers, they set out

LEFT: Neil was a devoted family man, seen here with his daughter Amber.

ABOVE: Neil and Pegi Young set up the pioneering Bridge School for handicapped children in 1984, appearing at a benefit concert every year.

to create a zero-emissions automobile that could run without roadside refuelling, and was suited economically for both long trips and short commutes. The project perfectly epitomized Young – slightly hairbrained, fearless, freethinking, ambitious, and environmental. It was an all-or-nothing labour of love driven by the audacity of hope.

The project started by converting a 1959 Lincoln Continental to have a hybrid engine that ran on electricity and biofuel. It was a classic US icon of power and oomph – a little rusty around the edges, tinkered into a healthy, eco-friendly, sustainable vision of the future – not unlike the man himself, some might say.

Along the way, there have been slight mishaps. In 2010, the car caught fire and inflamed a warehouse, causing $850,000 of damage, but – hey – this wouldn't be a Neil Young project if it wasn't self-destructive in some sort of way. His 2009 album *Fork in the Road* told the story in greater detail – chugging along to bluesy lo-fi riffs, laying down the project's ideals, and perpetuating Young's heartfelt stance that war, climate change, the economy, and most of the world's problems, are driven by an overwhelming dependence on oil.

Young spent much of the noughties turning into an angry, homespun pacifist with an iron will stubborn enough to make a difference.

One place where activism, eccentricities and an overwhelming spirit of rock come together perfectly is at the legendary Glastonbury Festival in the southwest of England, and Young was completely at home there when he headlined the event in 2009.

ABOVE: Young in 2005, after his brain aneurysm and father's death, ready to embark on a two-date performance of his *Prairie Wind* album, which resulted in a concert film directed Jonathan Demme.

RIGHT: Neil bosses day two of the Glastonbury festival at Worthy Farm, 2009.

Started by dairy farmer Michael Eavis in 1970 as a free festival replete with hippie ideals and free milk from the farm, nowadays 150,000 fans make an annual pilgrimage to the small village of Pilton in Somerset to see some of the world's biggest stars. Rejecting corporate sponsorship, and with an honourable history of raising millions of pounds for good causes, the site often becomes a muddy circus of strange sights such as naked Greenpeace protesters camping in teepees, gypsy communities, and tireless, drug fuelled techno-heads throwing shapes in the dance village. If any event retains a fragment of the Woodstock ethos, it is here.

From a lit-up Pyramid Stage, Young gazed out over a sea of people, flags, and campfires, and delivered one of his most memorable shows. Through plangent waves of roaring guitars, his career-spanning set of classic anthems came together with a mix of romance, idealism, and unbridled passion. Hunched over his Gibson Les Paul, peace signs adorning his guitar strap, Neil may have looked as though he had just wandered over from the Eavis' milking shed, but he set the night on fire, uniting the field for a mass singalong of "Heart of Gold", blazing away through countless reprises of "Rockin' in the Free World", and ending with a teary-eyed version of The Beatles' "A Day in the Life".

The next night, Bruce Springsteen followed with a highly polished, showbiz-tastic set of stadium rock anthems that had the farm jumpin' and a-hollerin', but it was Young who really captured the spirit of the festival.

LEFT: The man in black still taking no prisoners throughout the 2000s.

ABOVE: Preaching to the masses.

For a Hall of Fame rock icon burdened by having to live up to a reputation that he had earned in his youth, Young stood in stark contrast to previous headliners like the thumbs-in-the-air cheesy nostalgia of Paul McCartney and the plodding-through-the-motions "Hope I die, before I get old" embarrassment of The Who.

Unlike those two, Young may never be asked to provide the halftime entertainment at the Super Bowl – he's just too much of a risk; too odd; and has burnt too many bridges. But he'll never become a stale, dead-behind-the-eyes rock dinosaur, because what has always mattered to him is the music and the art form, and not the adoration or the fame.

Neil continues to display this insatiable hunger to play and create, complemented by a prolific output of challenging and provocative work. Neil did it again in 2010, when his album *Le Noise* distorted sonic boundaries by stripping his sound down to one raw, lonesome electric guitar. Working with Daniel Lanois – a producer famed for creating the lush, widescreen soundscapes of U2's *Joshua Tree* and *Achtung Baby* – the initial idea was to make a live acoustic album, free of overdubs and studio trickery. But things changed when Young strapped on his hollow-body White Falcon Gretsch, and started plugging in a bunch of effects pedals.

A sprawling, distorted growl of noise emerged as Young sang bygone tales wrought with road-worn memories, all delivered

PREVIOUS PAGE LEFT: Giddy career heights – Neil Young performs during the closing ceremony of the 2010 Winter Olympics in Vancouver as the Olympic Cauldron is extinguished.

PREVIOUS PAGE RIGHT: Neil at the 2011 Grammy Awards where he received his first Grammy for Best Rock Song for "Angry World".

in one or two takes. They were *Harvest*-style folk songs that changed into eerily melancholy, solo electric odes, free from the Crazy Horse rock 'n' roll influences that were once the man's trademark.

The track "Love and War" was a tapered-down example of acoustic minimalism – a beautifully maudlin anti-war ballad on which Young pondered his own career of protest songs. Then there was the Grammy-winning "Angry Man" that ploughed through layers of fuzz into a messy, noirish vision of the world.

The standout track, however, was the brilliant "Hitchhiker" that started off life as an unreleased song from 1992. The song found Young in reflective, autobiographical mood, surveying his glory days, settling old scores, and expressing cathartic gratitude for his good fortune. In it, he looks to his past, takes a deep breath, and waves on the future. Standing at the side of the road with his thumb out, he is ready for the next journey.

Who knows where that might lead? Not Neil Percival Young, that's for sure. He's heading down rock's highway with the wind flowing through his thinning hair in search of freedom and a better world for all. The eternal traveller rolls on his merry way with vegetable oil steaming out of his old '59 Lincoln, with grunge ghosts, folk dreams and rock anthems firmly locked in the trunk.

Hold on tight: the next turn could come at any moment and the road goes on forever.

ABOVE: Neil is joined onstage at his 2009 concert in London's Hyde Park by Paul McCartney for an epic performance of "A Day In The Life".

ABOVE LEFT: Neil appeared at the Canadian leg of the Live 8 concert in 2005 where he sang, among other things, "Four Strong Winds" with his wife Pegi, and "When God Made Me" backed by a gospel choir.